From *The Adventures of Hawk*:

Danny Hawk stepped up onto the windowsill and pressed himself against the glass and the corner of the stone wall. He was a solid five-foot-eight, and people called him husky. But luckily, the windowsill opening was just barely deep enough so that he wouldn't be seen if one of the killers looked his direction.

Now Danny just hoped no one below noticed him.

He kept himself perfectly still, using some of the techniques his Native American grandfather had taught him to stay calm.

"Like a stone," his grandfather would say. "Breathe in so slowly, no one can see you, exhale slowly, never stopping. Keep repeating to yourself: No one can see you."

Over and over, Danny did that, keeping himself pressed against the ledge and the glass, breathing as he had been taught.

Not moving.

I'm invisible. No one can see me.

Danny had never been so afraid in all his life.

His father had gone missing a month earlier, and now Professor Davis was killed because of Danny's father's notebooks.

What had his father found that had caused so much trouble?

Why did these men want that work?

Why was it so valuable?

And what was in the notebooks?

THE ADVENTURES OF HAWK

DEAN WESLEY SMITH

The Adventures of Hawk
Copyright © 2017 by Dean Wesley Smith
Published by WMG Publishing
Cover and interior design copyright © 2017 WMG Publishing
Cover art copyright © by Dmytro Denysov
ISBN-13: 978-1-56146-022-9
ISBN-10: 1-56146-022-2

ALSO BY DEAN WESLEY SMITH

Headed West: The Life and Times of Buffalo Jimmy

Life of a Dream

THE THUNDER MOUNTAIN SERIES:

Thunder Mountain

Monumental Summit

Avalanche Creek

The Edwards Mansion

Lake Roosevelt

Warm Springs

Melody Ridge

Grapevine Springs

The Idanha Hotel

The Taft Ranch

1

August 16, 1970
American University, Cairo, Egypt

Nineteen-year-old Danny Hawk held his breath and tried to listen. He had moved to a position near an open window in the old palace-like building that housed the science department of the American University in Cairo. Outside the window was a concrete ledge six inches wide. He could move along that ledge, three floors above the ground, if he had to.

From what he could hear, two men were threatening Professor Davis in the outer office. The professor was pretending that he had no idea what the men wanted, even though Danny knew that was a lie. The men were after Danny's father's records, just as Danny was.

"He's not going to tell us," one man's voice said. "Kill him and search the place. They have to be here."

There was a sound of scuffling and then a muffled gunshot.

Danny managed not to gasp or make any noise at all, but he wanted to be sick. It wasn't possible that Professor Davis had just been killed.

He couldn't be dead.

Danny's entire body felt like it had turned to Jell-O, but with more noise from the outer office, he made himself move.

And move quickly.

He climbed out the window and stood on the narrow ledge. Holding on to the rough wall as best he could, he pulled the window silently closed behind him. The only other exit out of that back office was through where the professor had just been killed, and Danny certainly wasn't going that way.

The late-evening Cairo air was hot and dry. A slight wind whipped at his loose pants and shirt as he stood with his back against the stone wall. His long black hair blew around his face as he edged inch-by-inch along the stone ledge. He had spent a lot of time climbing rocks back home in Idaho and he had no fear of heights.

But his life also hadn't been threatened in any of those climbing expeditions.

And none of them had been on the side of a building.

He forced himself to concentrate on what he was doing and try to not think about what had just happened inside.

The lights of the massive city of Cairo spread out in front of him. From the ledge, he had a good view over the palm trees and buildings, and in the distance, the Pyramids at Giza were lit up. There was so much light in the downtown area, he felt like there was a spotlight on him. The last thing he needed was to be seen from below and attention drawn to what he was doing.

The door slammed open to the back office and the men's voices got louder.

"Search it and make sure you don't miss anything."

Danny glanced back. Through the edge of the window, he caught a glimpse of a man with a red hood wearing the traditional Arab robe. Except for two eye-holes, his face was completely covered, but Danny caught a glimpse of one of the man's hands. His skin was so pale, he couldn't be Arab. And he had a tattoo on his hand that looked like something with a snake.

Danny glanced away from the window at his path of escape ahead. This wall of the American University Science Building was long, with evenly spaced windows along the ledge. He didn't dare try for the corner. That was too far, and would risk him being seen from either the men in the office or someone on the ground below.

Either would likely get him killed.

The next window to a dark office was locked. Danny glanced back. If one of the men happened to open the window and look outside, he would see Danny.

Danny stepped up onto the windowsill and pressed himself against the glass and the corner of the stone wall. He was a solid five-foot-eight, and people called him husky. But luckily, the windowsill opening was just barely deep enough so that he wouldn't be seen if one of the men looked his direction.

Now Danny just hoped no one below noticed him.

He kept himself perfectly still, using some of the techniques his Native American grandfather had taught him to stay calm.

"Like a stone," his grandfather would say. "Breathe in so slowly, no one can see you, exhale slowly, never stopping. Keep repeating to yourself: No one can see you."

Over and over, Danny did that, keeping himself pressed against the ledge and the glass, breathing as he had been taught.

Not moving.

I'm invisible. No one can see me.

Danny had never been so afraid in all his life.

His father had gone missing a month earlier, and now Professor Davis was killed because of Danny's father's notebooks.

What had his father found that had caused so much trouble?

Why did these men want that work?

Why was it so valuable?

And what was in the notebooks?

Danny had no answers to any of those questions. The last couple of years, his father had been gone so much, they hadn't talked.

But whatever it was in those notebooks to make them so valuable, if Danny wasn't careful, he would be killed as well for it, before he had any chance to find out what was going on, or what had happened to his father.

His mother insisted that his father was still alive, that she would know in her heart, in her very soul, if he had been killed. And Danny trusted that special connection. His father was being held somewhere. Maybe close by in this very city, as far as Danny knew.

That's why Danny, his best friend, Craig, and his Uncle Steve were in Cairo. The authorities didn't seem to care what had happened to Danny's father, so now he had to go in search.

Danny had expected that his father's notebooks, left with Professor Davis days before his father disappeared, might give him a clue to what had happened.

He never expected the notebooks themselves to get someone killed.

Finally, he heard a clear voice from Professor Davis's office. "There's nothing here."

"Wipe up the blood," another voice said. "Wrap the professor in his rug. We'll haul him with us and make sure his body is very lost in the desert."

The sound of movement echoed out over the night, then one of the men asked the other.

"What do we do now?"

"We trail Hawk's kid," the voice said. "He'll lead us right to the notebooks. His father must have told him where they were. Of that, I'm sure."

Danny was startled at the mention of him. How did these killers know he was in Cairo?

He forced himself to stay perfectly still, to breathe regularly. The last thing he needed at this point, on this ledge, was to panic.

"The kid's here in Cairo?" the other man asked.

"Yeah, he flew in this morning with a friend and Professor Hawk's brother. No reason for them to be here except to find the professor and get his notebooks. Those three will be easy pickings."

Danny was stunned breathless.

Whoever those two men were, they had just confirmed that they were after his father's notebooks. And they knew that Craig and Uncle Steve had come with him to Cairo.

The other man laughed. "Yeah, who knows, we might not have to even kill the three of them."

"Don't count on it," the man in charge said.

2

August 16, 1970
American University, Cairo, Egypt

Danny Hawk waited long enough on the ledge to make sure the men had gone, then when the area below the window was clear of late-night walkers, he eased along the ledge and back inside Professor Davis's darkened back office.

He didn't dare turn on the light. His eyes were accustomed to the dark anyway, so he pulled the window closed and locked it, and then moved quickly over to where Professor Davis had hung his suit coat on the inside door of the closet. Luckily, the coat was still right there.

In the dim light, the room didn't look like it had been searched. Clearly these men were professionals.

Danny wanted, more than anything, to just take his uncle and Craig and head for the airport, go home and forget all of this. Whatever his father had found had gotten him either killed or taken captive. And now it had gotten Professor Davis killed as well. And there was no telling how many other lives had been lost.

Danny knew, without a doubt, that he was in far, far over his head.

And there was no one to turn to, no one to trust. The only contact they had had in Cairo had just been killed.

Now it was up to him to get his uncle and Craig to safety and quickly. If there was a safe place anywhere in the world.

The professor's suit coat was the reason that Danny had been in the back office in the first place. The professor's car keys were in his suit coat pocket, and Danny, on Professor Davis's instructions, had gone to get them just as those men had burst into the front office. The professor had told Danny that the notebooks were in the trunk of his car in the faculty parking garage.

Danny searched the pockets of Professor Davis's suit jacket, feeling very odd that he was searching through a dead man's clothing. He pushed that thought back and finally came up with the keys.

He put them in his pocket and moved silently toward the door to the outer office. He opened it carefully, and silently, only a crack. The office was empty, the lights off. It looked cleaned and everything in place.

There was no body.

The rug that had been under Professor Davis's chair was missing. Otherwise, everything looked to be in order. Someone coming in would think the professor hadn't been here. It would be days before anyone reported him missing, since he wasn't married.

Danny moved over to the phone and started to call his uncle at the hotel. Danny couldn't go back there, and he now had to get his uncle and his best friend, Craig James, out of there as well without them being seen.

Then, before he had finished dialing the number, he stopped and put the phone back in the cradle, looking at it as if it were a snake that might bite him at any moment.

"Think," he said softly to himself. "Come on, think."

He forced himself to take two slow, deep breaths, let his mind clear a little.

"Those men are professionals. That phone could be tapped."

He took a few more deep breaths just as his grandfather had

trained him to do, and tried to put himself into the mind of a criminal who didn't want to get caught. He'd read enough mystery novels that he should be able to do that.

And right now, he and his uncle and best friend needed to completely vanish from all sight in Africa's largest city.

And quickly.

Danny looked around the dimly lit office. What had he touched?

He took a couple of Kleenex tissues from a box on the professor's desk, then wiped his fingerprints off of the phone. And along the edge of the desk. Then he went back into the inner office and wiped down anything he might have touched in there, including the window. If the professor's body was discovered, there was no point in being connected to this in any way. And since he had an Egyptian visa, he had been fingerprinted when they entered the country.

When he finished, he made himself stand in the center of each room and look around, going over all his movements. He didn't dare miss anything.

"Look carefully," he muttered. "Very carefully."

He then made sure that any surface he might have even accidentally touched was wiped clean. Except for the outer doorknob of the office door, he was finally convinced that he had cleaned off every trace that he had been in the office.

He went out into the hallway and finished the doorknob, then put the tissue in his pocket.

The hallway had very high ceilings and was as wide as some streets. The floor was marble and polished. He walked silently along the empty hall, acting as if he were just a student here who had come later in the evening to see a professor, even though his heart felt like it wanted to explode out of his chest.

So much for the old Indian ways in keeping himself calm. Now he wished he had spent even more time with his grandfather before he died and learned more about self-control. It just never seemed like he would need it. At least, not like this.

He used the wide staircase in the old building and went down to the second floor. An empty receptionist desk filled a large area near the wide marble staircase. A public use phone sat on top of the desk and Danny picked it up and was quickly connected to his hotel.

The hotel was massive and modern. It looked out over the Nile River. Even their room had a river view. They had all been excited getting to it after the long plane flight. Now they were all going to have to run from it, and fast.

His uncle, Steve Hawk, answered the phone. Uncle Steve was the exact opposite of Danny's father. He was friendly, liked to stay at home, and wasn't very smart. Even he admitted that when they had passed out the brains between him and Danny's father, he had got a half serving.

Craig and Danny had the room next door to Uncle Steve's room. Craig was much taller than Danny, standing just over six feet. He had blonde hair and a smile that never seemed to quit. He lived in the same small ski town in central Idaho and his father tried to run a restaurant for tourists, but he drank more than he worked. During the summer for the past few years, Craig had helped Danny and his uncle on their tourist boat on the big mountain lake just to get away from his father.

To Danny, Uncle Steve had been there for him far more than his world-traveling archeologist father had ever been. And even when his father was at home, he was always up north at the University of Idaho, doing research and getting ready for his next trip.

"Uncle Steve," Danny said quickly when he answered the phone. "Don't say anything, just listen to me. I need you and Craig to meet me at the south entrance of the U.S. Embassy. Go down a back staircase and out a hotel back door. Make sure you are not followed. Bring your luggage and what you can of my stuff as well. You're never going back to those rooms. If I'm not there beside the embassy, wait for me without being seen. Move fast. Your lives are in danger."

Then Danny hung up without giving his uncle a chance to argue. More than likely, the call had just scared the poor man half to death. And that was good. After what Danny had just been through, they all needed to be scared if they were going to have any chance of surviving.

Danny forced himself to take another deep breath and think about staying calm.

The seemingly empty old building loomed around him. He had read that a long time ago this building had housed the University of Cairo, before that school moved across the river to larger grounds. It had been some sort of ancient palace before that.

He stood silently, working to calm his racing heart. No one seemed to be listening, to even know he was there. But after what happened to Professor Davis, he could never completely trust that feeling again. He was going to have to be careful every moment and try not to do anything too stupid.

What he really wanted to do was call the police and then just curl up behind the desk until they arrived. But he couldn't do that either. He was in Egypt. A country that was going through a change of government and unrest. Nassar, the leader since 1952, had just died and a man by the name of Sadat looked like he was going to take control. The last thing Danny needed was to get involved with the Egyptian police at this point. Instead of trying to find his father, he might spend the next year in a jail cell even though he hadn't done anything.

Danny had no doubt at all that the three of them were very much on their own. And next what he had to do was take a huge risk and get his father's notebooks out of the trunk of Professor Davis's car. Those notebooks were the only chance he had of finding out exactly what was happening.

And why his father had disappeared and Professor Davis had been killed.

3

August 16, 1970
American University parking garage, Cairo, Egypt

Danny moved silently into the two-story parking garage and up to the second floor where Professor Davis had said his small red sedan was parked. The car was tiny compared to American cars, but after spending only a half-day so far in Cairo, Danny understood why all the cars here were small. The streets were jam-packed and, except for the main boulevards, as narrow as an alley. You had to have a small car to even get around.

He stood to one side of the garage in a deep shadow and just watched and waited.

Nothing was moving at all.

But he didn't trust that.

He stayed there, silently in the dark, watching, listening, breathing slowly and deeply as his grandfather had taught him.

No movement.

Nothing.

Finally, he stepped forward as if he belonged there, walking with the gait of someone who was heading to his car to go home.

The key fit perfectly in the trunk of the car, even though Danny's hands were shaking.

The trunk looked empty.

Danny's stomach twisted. Oh, no! Had he heard the professor wrong?

Or had someone else gotten to the notebooks first?

He dug in the trunk, moving first an old blanket and then the spare tire. In the well under the tire, was a dark blue backpack, blending into the bottom of the trunk.

Danny recognized his father's brown notebooks inside. Six of them.

He replaced the tire and blanket, made sure the backpack was securely closed, then put it over his shoulder.

He finished his search of the trunk, finding nothing more that belonged to his father.

Using the tissue still in his pocket, he wiped off his fingerprints from everything he had touched, including the trunk lid, then unlocked the front door, wiped off the keys as well, and tossed them in the tray between the seats.

He quickly locked the door again, closed it as silently as he could, and then turned and walked away toward a side entrance.

He was sweating, his hands were shaking, and his breath was coming fast and hard. What he had taken from the car belonged to him, his father's notebooks, and Danny had had permission to get into the car. Yet, it still felt as if he had just robbed something.

And with Professor Davis dead, Danny would have a very hard time proving that he hadn't robbed the car.

Or, for that matter, killed the professor. Who would believe his story of a red-hooded man?

This garage in Cairo, Egypt, was a long way from the tree-covered mountains of central Idaho where he had grown up, and the tourist boat his mother and Uncle Steve ran.

In two weeks, he was supposed to start back at Boise State University in his second year, and even though he got good grades, he didn't work hard at it. He was much more worried about what was going to happen in two years when he graduated with a degree in English. He didn't really believe in all the fighting and killing going on in Vietnam, so for the moment staying in college was the best thing he could do.

All of it seemed so overwhelming to face.

At least, until his father had disappeared and the next thing Danny knew, he was trying to stay alive in a parking garage in Cairo, Egypt. Worrying about being drafted into the Vietnam War suddenly seemed very tame.

At the edge of the garage, Danny opened the door to the staircase, then let it close without going through. He stayed in the shadows, listening, watching for any movement at all in the garage. He needed to know if he had been followed out of the main building.

He stood perfectly still, his jeans and dark shirt blending into the shadows.

Nothing was moving.

The warm wind blew strange city smells through the garage, and in the distance, sirens cut through the night sounds.

Finally convinced that he hadn't been followed to the car, he walked down the curling ramp to the ground level and out the main entrance, turning toward the U.S. Embassy.

He kept one hand on the backpack strap as he turned south on a wide boulevard, trying to keep his pace the same as the few other walkers out this late at night. He knew he looked like a tourist of some sort or another. His long black hair and dark complexion from his Native American heritage helped him blend in a little, but not much.

He forced himself to keep an eye on everything as he walked.

No one seemed to be paying him any attention, but he had to be sure. Even though the American University was in the same general area of Cairo as the U.S. Embassy, he still had almost a mile to walk. Cairo was a huge city, the biggest in Africa. And Craig and his Uncle had a good mile to travel from the hotel to the embassy as well, coming from the north along the river.

He stopped two blocks from the embassy, ducked into an open restaurant and then stood out of sight near the front door, making sure no one was following him.

No one was, at least that he could see. But he was convinced that someone with real skill could be following him easily, and he would never know it.

If that were the case, he was as good as dead.

Finally, after waiting long enough to give himself a little confidence that he was alone, he went the last few blocks to the south side of the U.S. Embassy.

Craig and his uncle were standing hidden from the street between a fruit stand and a dark alley.

Danny walked up in front of them, then pointed at the street as a black and white taxi approached. He had been told that was what he needed to do to catch a cab in the city, but he hadn't tried it yet. The taxi slowed, its window down.

"Airport!" Danny shouted at the driver, and the driver pulled over to the curb quickly.

Danny kept the backpack on his shoulder while, without a word, his Uncle and Craig loaded the bags they had brought into the trunk and back seat of the small Fiat taxi.

Danny slid in beside the driver, indicating that no one should say a word. In broken English, and what little Arabic Danny knew, he and the driver worked out a fare by the time they were halfway to their destination. Six Egyptian pounds. That was just under two dollars U.S. Danny knew that was high, but at the moment, he didn't care.

He had the cab driver leave them at the international terminal, then Danny led the way inside and to a hidden restaurant off to one side of a large concourse.

After they were settled at the table, Uncle Steve turned to Danny. "All right, you want to tell us why you scared us to death and brought us here?"

Danny took a deep breath and let himself relax a little for the first time in the last two hours. He figured he might as well tell them the important detail first, then fill in the rest later.

"Professor Davis was killed tonight by two professional killers looking for my father's notebooks."

Both Uncle Steve and Craig stared at him with their mouths open. If it hadn't been so serious, it might have been funny.

"They're going to come after us next to find them," Danny said. "And they will kill us to get the notebooks. Actually, more than likely, they will kill us anyhow."

"Oh," Uncle Steve said, his face suddenly drained of any sign of color.

"And we have them?" Craig asked.

Danny patted the backpack he had on the floor beside his chair. "We have them."

"Oh, great, now what are we going to do?" Uncle Steve asked, his face white.

"Get on an airplane and get out of here," Craig said. "I'll even buy the tickets."

Craig stood up and reached for his wallet. "I think I have enough money."

Danny shook his head. "Nope."

Craig dropped back into his chair. "How did I know you were going to say that?"

"We're not leaving?" Uncle Steve asked, his voice cracking.

"Nope," Danny said. "We're going to find a safe hotel and hole up while we read my father's notebooks. Then we're going to do what we came here to do."

"Find out what happened to your father," Craig said.

"Exactly," Danny said. "And besides, we can't go home. They would just go there and kill us, and maybe my mother, and there is no way I'm putting her in danger."

He looked around at the three of them. "I heard the men talking about when we arrived in town and how easy we would be to deal with. These people are very real and connected and they seem to have eyes everywhere. We have to find out what they want and why. We're the only hope my father has at this moment."

"So we're committed to this search," Craig said.

"Very," Danny said.

Uncle Steve didn't say anything. He just looked like he might be sick at any moment.

4

August 17, 1970
Gizera Hotel, Cairo, Egypt

Making sure that they weren't followed, Danny Hawk, his best friend, Craig, and his Uncle Steve left the airport restaurant and hailed a cab to a hotel that Danny had found a small ad for in the airport. It was on the west side of the river on Gizera Avenue. The hotel was spread out around a number of courtyards, each filled with decorative rock and a few palm trees and nothing more. It wasn't an upscale tourist hotel, but it wasn't bad. It looked like it catered more to businessmen from the area.

The area smelled lightly of dirty water and animals. Not at all a smell Danny would have expected in the center of a big city.

Again, they got a room for Uncle Steve while Danny and Craig shared a room with two beds. They registered under false names, booking the room for three days. The night clerk had been so tired, he hadn't even asked to see their identification or passports like the bigger hotel had done.

Craig just passed out, snoring lightly, his six-foot-plus frame dangling over the edge of the bed, but Danny didn't sleep much during what was left of the night. But he managed to rest and think. So by breakfast in the small hotel restaurant, he was feeling more in control.

Scared and completely over his head, but in control.

The men who were looking for them would have no way of tracing them through the thousands of hotels in Cairo. More than likely, they were still watching the Continental where they had been staying. And would for a few days at least, since Uncle Steve had paid for three nights and they hadn't checked out when they left.

"What's the plan this morning?" Craig asked Danny.

"We should contact the authorities," Uncle Steve said, using his confident voice. The voice Danny knew he always used when trying to get something from someone.

"And say what?" Danny asked, staring at his uncle. Sitting in the airport restaurant last night, he had told them the entire story of how he managed to escape and get the notebooks.

Uncle Steve looked flustered, his face growing slightly red which was accented by his gray hair. "I don't know, but we should."

"For all we know," Danny said, "the police were who killed Professor Davis."

Uncle Steve started to say something, but Danny held up his hand. "We don't know, do we?"

Uncle Steve just shrugged.

"We're not in the United States, remember." Danny patted the backpack he had carried with him from the room. "And we have no idea just what's in these notebooks or how valuable they are."

"Valuable enough to kill for," Craig said, shaking his head and looking worried. "That's for sure. We need to read them, find out why."

"Agreed," Danny said. "And that's the plan for the day."

After breakfast, they went back to Uncle Steve's room.

When Danny opened the first book bound in leather and full of his father's writings, he was almost instantly disappointed. This was going to be a lot more difficult than he had thought.

The notebooks were in a combination of English, Italian, Latin, and Egyptian hieroglyphs. Danny knew his father was fluent in all four languages, plus a few others, including some Arabic, since he had worked so often in Egypt. Clearly, he had no trouble writing in all the languages as well and had done so from one paragraph to another, changing without any seeming reason.

Danny knew some Latin and some French, but that was all. Not much help.

"Who can read what language?" Danny asked, handing the notebook to Craig and picking up another to see if it was the same. It was.

"A little Spanish," Craig said, shrugging.

"Nothing," Uncle Steve said, looking apologetic. "It would figure my brother would protect his notes with something like this. He always did like to show off how smart he was."

Danny ignored the old family chant he had heard his uncle say hundreds of times. "Well, let's read what we can and figure out how to get help with what we can't read later."

Danny took back the first notebook and started into the record of the last ten years of his father's research. It felt like reading his father's private thoughts was snooping on something his father had never wanted him to see.

Three hours later, Danny put down the last notebook and sat back, trying to make sense of what he had been able to read.

It seemed that his father had been focused on finding archeological records of what he had started to call "The Fountain." That was short for the Fountain of Youth.

Danny had been around his father and his work enough to know that with any myth coming up through history, there was usually some sort of factual basis somewhere in the past. His father clearly didn't believe in any water that could keep a person youthful, so he was searching for the start of the myth.

And why the myth existed the way it did.

Somewhere, in the second year, the word Taccola had come into the notebooks. Danny knew a little about Taccola because his father had been so interested in him when Danny was ten. Taccola was an engineer in the late fourteen century in Siena, and his inventions were amazingly ahead of their time. Many of the inventions concerned moving water to the city of Siena, which was a landlocked city without a good water supply.

But later in Taccola's life, he had been interested in finding older inventions and had led expeditions into parts of Egypt, where he vanished without a trace somewhere around 1458.

His father had underlined a phrase that bothered Danny a great deal. "Could Taccola still be alive?"

That was the last mention of Taccola in the notebooks, at least in the parts that Danny could read.

The next book dealt with Napoleon's interest in ancient culture and the archeological searches he funded and went on in Egypt and other areas around the Mediterranean. It seemed that, as with Taccola, Napoleon was focused on water in his searches, possibly even something that was rumored to give his men an invincibility.

At one point, his father had written "He was searching for the Fountain."

It was in the fourth journal that the words *Hydra Journals* were written, then underlined.

Danny couldn't tell from what he could read in English what the Hydra Journals were about, but from that point onward, they seemed to be a focus for his father. Five years of intense focus, as a matter of fact, from what Danny could tell from the dates in the notebooks.

The very last entry in the last notebook had been in English. It had basically said that Danny's father had made a breakthrough, but somehow he was going to have to keep his find from the *Hydra League*.

Then he wrote a few notes in Egyptian hieroglyph and the journal ended.

From the last date in the notebook, Danny's father had taken them to Professor Davis for safekeeping the next day and then vanished two days later.

Danny stared at the words *Hydra League*.

Was the red-hooded man who killed Professor Davis part of that league?

Was it the league that had taken his father?

Hydra, an old Greek legend was about a snake with many women's heads.

Hydra Journals. Water. Fountain of Youth. Taccola. Napoleon. Hydra League.

Danny sighed, sat back, and closed his eyes while Craig and Uncle Steve kept reading.

At least he knew a little more of where his father's research had taken him. But now Danny was more confused and scared than he had been last night.

And he had no idea what to do next.

5

August 18, 1970
Gizera Hotel, Cairo, Egypt

They had spent the entire previous day reading what they could of the notebooks a second time and talking about them and what they contained. They hadn't left the hotel and had turned in early to get rested, with the understanding that at breakfast they would decide what to do next.

Danny barely slept, even though he was exhausted. Every time he closed his eyes, a red-hooded snake with many heads would come up out of a black pool of water and chase him.

He wasn't sure he was having a vision dream, as his grandfather would sometimes call vivid images like that, or just a nightmare. Danny had a hunch it was a little bit of both.

But he did know that he was his father's only chance of survival if he was still alive.

And Danny had to believe his mother that his father was alive. Somewhere, being held by someone.

And now, just like his father, Danny was in too deep. There was no turning back, no going home, back to the easy life of going to school.

Across the restaurant table the next morning, Danny looked at his best friend and his uncle, then laid out simply what he thought they should do next.

"Uncle Steve, Craig, I want you two to take a flight from here to London, then on home."

"What?" Craig asked.

Danny held up his hand. "Let me finish. Uncle Steve, I need you to get my mother out on your boat into the upper areas of the lake. The old cabin up on the point should be safe for a time. Lock up the house and just go, get on that boat and stay away from contact as much as possible.

Uncle Steve shook his head and Craig looked disgusted.

"We're not leaving you," Craig said. "And who do I have to go home to? My drunken father?"

Danny knew Craig was right. There was no one at home for Craig. His mother was dead and his father spent more time in bars than at home. Craig pretended to live with his father, but in reality, he spent most of his time at Danny's house. Not only were they best friends, but Craig was like the brother Danny never had. And Danny's mother considered him her second son.

"Your mother would kill me if I left her son over here alone," Uncle Steve said. "And she'd have a right to."

"Uncle Steve," Danny said, "the men who took my father, and who killed Professor Davis, are not going to stop at the border of Egypt. They know we're here, they know we left my mother alone. Once they can't find us, where do you think they're going to go next?"

Uncle Steve's skin turned a sickly white and he instantly started sweating. He clearly hadn't thought of that.

Danny stared into the fear-filled eyes of his uncle. "Someone needs to protect my mother, and you're the best man for that. Get out on the boat on that lake and up to the cabin on the point."

"But you can't stay here alone," Uncle Steve said.

"He's not going to be alone," Craig said, his voice full of anger. "I'm staying with him and there's no argument on that point."

Danny looked at his best friend, then smiled. He had been hoping that Craig would say that. Together, they had more of a chance than Danny did alone, that was for sure.

Craig then turned to Uncle Steve. "But Danny's right, you have to go back and get his mother safe."

Uncle Steve sighed and slumped in the booth.

Danny knew that he had put his uncle in an impossible situation. He either had to leave two boys he still considered his "babies" in danger in a foreign country, or he had to live with the fact that if he didn't go back, Danny's mother more than likely would be killed.

"Remember," Danny said, "we may be young, but we are considered adults. We'll be fine."

Uncle Steve didn't even nod at that, just stared down at his hands.

"One other thing," Danny said. "We're going to need money at times if we're going to try to find out what happened to my father and stay hidden from the men after the notebooks. Craig and I can live pretty cheap here, and stay out of sight easier if it's just the two of us than if you are with us. But even still, we're going to need someone we can contact for money."

Uncle Steve again just sighed, but this time he nodded as well.

Danny knew that his uncle had a pretty good sum of money stashed from the settlement from his wife's death.

"You're going to be our anchor," Danny said. "You and my mother have to stay safe, and yet be in contact with us. And from the looks of these notebooks, there's no telling where this is going to take us, or how long it's going to take."

Craig laughed. "I suddenly feel like I've been tossed into a quest fantasy."

"I just wish this was a fantasy," Danny said, smiling at his friend. "It's just a little too real and deadly for my tastes."

"No argument there," Craig said.

6

August 19, 1970
International Airport, Cairo, Egypt

Late that night, just after midnight, the three of them went back to the international airport. Uncle Steve booked them all tickets to London, then on to Seattle. From there Uncle Steve would drive back to central Idaho. The idea was that if the men who were after the notebooks thought all three of them had left, they would follow Uncle Steve to Seattle.

"Are you sure you want them after you?" Danny had asked his uncle when he suggested the idea.

Uncle Steve nodded. "Don't worry, they'll never find your mother and me after we get on that lake. The old cabin has no entrance road and no one really remembers it's out there. Besides, looking for you in Seattle will keep them off your trail here for a while at least."

Danny didn't like it, but he had agreed to the plan.

The plane didn't leave until six in the morning, so for the rest of the night, the three of them sat in a secluded place where they could see people in the international airport coming and going. They planned as much as they could during those hours, including how and when Danny and Craig would check in with Uncle Steve and his mother.

The first thing Danny and Craig had to do was try to get new identification. Uncle Steve left them with enough money to last them for a few months in Cairo, and they set up how more money could be wired to them.

As Uncle Steve got ready to go through customs, he turned to Danny. "You're mother's going to kill me, you know."

Danny laughed. "Just make her close up the house and get away from there."

"Oh, I will," Uncle Steve said, the worry in his lined face clear. "Twelve hours after I reach home, we'll be gone."

"Good," Danny said. He gave his uncle a hug, then Craig did the same.

"Be careful," Uncle Steve said. "And find my brother, would you?"

"We will," Craig said for both of them.

Uncle Steve nodded, then with a worried smile turned and headed into the customs area.

Danny and Craig stood off to one side, watching all the people coming and going through that area of the airport. No one seemed to be paying them any attention, so after a good half hour, they went out the door and took a cab into the old heart of Cairo, right to the Khan Al-Khalili bazaar.

Neither of them spoke on their ride into the center of the city. Danny felt completely overwhelmed by what they faced, and very much afraid. Chances were he and Craig would be killed far before they found Danny's father. But they had to try.

They had no other choice.

7

August 19, 1970
Khan Al-Khalili bazaar, Cairo, Egypt

Stepping out of the modern city of Cairo and into the bazaar was like stepping through time back centuries, much like turning off a modern boulevard in New Orleans and going into the French Quarter. The narrow streets were jammed with everything imaginable being sold on both sides, and the noise level was intense, with people bargaining for everything, often at the top of their lungs.

Ancient two-story buildings and many cloth overhangs and tents kept out the early morning sunlight, making the long, crowded market seem like a carnival without any lights turned on. From what Danny understood, it was this crowded all morning and into the early afternoon every day. At least for now, the shade kept the temperature down. Later this afternoon, with the sun directly overhead, this street would be almost too hot to walk on.

"Oh, wow, does that smell good," Craig said, walking past a booth where a woman was cooking something in a large pot.

It did smell wonderful, like a combination of beef stew and baking bread, but Danny wasn't sure if he was up to eating from a street vender just yet, even though he was starting to get a little hungry.

They passed one booth after another, all cooking something different. And the cooking smells mixed with the smells of incense and new rugs hanging from almost everything.

The booth and the crowds stretched as far as Danny could see, and the moment they got into the crowds, he became separated from Craig for a moment. After they got back together, they agreed that if they did get separated, they would meet back on the corner where the cab had just let them off.

"So, where do we start?" Craig asked.

Danny looked at the crowds and booths selling food, incense, rugs, lamps, and just about everything else. "I don't have a clue. Let's just walk and see what we see."

They were looking for help with languages reading the journals, and Uncle Steve had suggested that the best place to find help, and maybe a guide to the city, was at the famous bazaar. So it was the first thing Danny and Craig were going to try.

They had walked the crowded street for most of an hour, not even beginning to see all of the bazaar yet, when a short, young Arab man approached them and motioned that they should move to the edge of the street, near a building, so they could talk.

The guy was short, no more than five-three, and both Danny and Craig towered over him. He looked to be about their age, maybe younger, and had a robe on that clearly had seen better days. He wore the traditional sandals of the city, and nothing on his thick, unruly black hair.

As they got to a place near a building wall where the crowd wouldn't bang at them like a river trying to go around a rock, the guy said, "American tourists?" He spoke in clear English with a slight British accent that seemed really odd coming from a short Arab boy in ragged robes.

Danny nodded.

The guy introduced himself, rattling off a name that was long, complex, and that Danny had no chance of following. Then he smiled and said, "But my American friends all call me 'Bud'."

"Nice meeting you, Bud," Danny said without giving him their names.

Bud looked at each of them, then shrugged. "You looked like you were looking for something since you entered the bazaar. I just thought I'd offer my services in finding what you are searching after."

Danny felt a shock of fear hit him, and clearly Craig wasn't happy with the sound of that either. This guy named Bud had been following them since they entered the bazaar and they *hadn't* noticed. And Danny had been watching for anyone following them.

"You were following us?" Craig asked, sounding as worried as Danny felt.

Bud shrugged, his tattered robe moving like waves on a calm sea. "Sure. You looked like you needed help. That's what I do, I offer my help."

"For a fee," Craig said.

Bud smiled. "Of course. But it is a very *small* fee."

"I'll bet," Craig said.

"Was anyone else following us?" Danny asked.

"No," Bud said. "I would have seen them. Were you expecting someone to be?"

"We're hoping not," Danny said. "But for all we know, you were paid by the people looking for us to follow us."

Bud laughed. "Oh, trust me, anyone could have followed you. They would not have needed to hire me."

Danny had to agree the short guy was right. He was starting to think that this guy might be able to help them, or at least, for a small fee, point them in the right direction.

"Do you know the city well?" Danny asked.

Bud laughed. "I have survived on these streets since I was ten. Of course I do. The streets are my home."

"Can you read other languages besides Arabic and English?" Craig asked.

"Some Italian, some French," Bud said, now looking puzzled. It was clearly not a question that he had been expecting.

Danny glanced at Craig, who nodded.

"Can you find us someone who also can read Latin and knows some hieroglyphs?"

Bud again shrugged. "Of course."

"Can you wait here for a moment," Danny asked Bud. "I need to talk to my friend."

Danny and Craig stepped a half dozen steps away. "He might be exactly what we're looking for to start with," Danny said.

"As long as you keep an eye on your wallet at all times," Craig said, "I agree."

Then he smiled the devious smile that Danny had come to know over the years. It was a smile that tended to get them into trouble more than anything else.

"How about we make up some sort of treasure?" Craig said. "Tell him that we're searching for it, and offer to let him join us. That way he's got a stake in it as well and won't charge us when he helps us."

"You mean like the Hydra Journals and the Fountain of Youth?" Danny asked, smiling.

"Yeah, that treasure," Craig said, laughing. "I guess we really are after a treasure, aren't we?"

Danny nodded. "I have a hunch we find those Hydra Journals, we find my father."

"I bet you're right," Craig said. "And let's just hope the Fountain of Youth is real as well."

"So," Danny said, "let's hire this Bud to help us find someone else to do languages, tell him we're in danger and ask him what he suggests for places to live and hide, and then if we like him, we'll tell him everything."

"A good plan," Craig said.

Together, they returned to Bud, who had been leaning against a building, waiting and watching things around them. He seemed almost invisible, he blended in so well. And his eyes didn't seem to miss anything. Danny didn't know why, exactly, but he trusted this guy. He just hoped he and Craig wouldn't pay later for that trust.

"We'll talk money in a few minutes," Danny said to Bud, "but we first need to know if you can get us to someone who can read Latin and hieroglyphs."

"Sure," Bud said. "The twins. They're staying in a small apartment near here."

"Twins?" Danny asked.

"Ernie and Ed," Bud said, shrugging. "That's more than likely not their real names, but that's what they go by here. They're from South Africa and have skin as black as the night. They say they're traveling the world searching for treasures, but I think they're trying to escape something."

"How old are they?" Craig asked.

"You two look about twenty," Bud said. "The twins are about your ages I'd say, but they've never told me."

Danny was shocked at how smart this short guy was.

"How old are you?" Craig asked.

The guy shrugged. "I am close to your age, but I have lived a long time in those short years."

Danny didn't doubt that at all. "How do you know these twins can read Latin?"

"Because I watched them one day in an old palace underground near here. They're the smartest two people I've ever met."

Danny looked at Craig, who nodded.

Danny turned back to Bud. "Can you help us find a place to live that will be hidden from those chasing us?"

"Sure," Bud said. "Where are you living now?"

"A hotel," Danny said, not wanting to give him the actual name just yet.

"Real tourists," Bud said. He looked at Danny, then at Craig. "But you're here alone?"

Danny nodded.

"And someone might be following you and you need a place to live and hide while you translate some sort of language problem. Right?"

"Right," Danny said, knowing exactly what Bud was doing. He was starting to bargain for a rate to help them. "Twenty pounds for the day for you to help us."

"Fifty," Bud said. "And if you don't like the twins, I'll find you someone else."

"Thirty," Danny said, "and not a penny more."

"Thirty-five or you find yourself another guide. And you have to show me you have that much on you."

"Deal," Danny said, flashing a fifty-pound note. "And if you do us a good job today, we may have another offer for you after we're finished."

Bud smiled. "I like the sound of that. What first? A safe place to live or meet the twins?"

"The twins," Danny said and Craig nodded.

"Follow me," Bud said and turned, almost vanishing into the crowds of shoppers at once.

Danny quickly checked his wallet. It was still there. He had a hunch that with Bud, he would be checking for his wallet all the time.

8

August 19, 1970
Khan Al-Khalili bazaar, Cairo, Egypt

Bud had to wait for them a number of times in the short two blocks through the bazaar to an ancient stone building on the right of the street. The heat of the day was increasing by the minute and Danny not only found himself even more hungry than he had been earlier, but also sweating.

Craig was sweating as well. They needed to get out of the heat pretty soon and get something to drink. The Pacific Northwest just didn't have this kind of dry heat.

When Bud finally stopped and waited for them one last time, he said as Danny stopped in front of him, "We're going to have to get you both some better clothes for this heat and not being followed. You stand out like a fire on a dark night."

Danny nodded. He had thought of that, but hadn't expected Bud to.

"Wait here," Bud said, indicating a place still in the shade against a building. "I'll see if they are home and if they are interested in seeing you."

With that, Bud turned and disappeared through an archway that led somewhere into the shadows of the buildings.

"We're going to need food and water pretty soon," Craig said.

Danny nodded. "Bud can tell us which booth is safe to eat at."

"If you buy him lunch," Craig said, laughing.

Danny had no doubt he was going to have to do that. Luckily for them, the exchange rate made staying here very cheap. The thirty-five pounds he had offered Bud for his services was less than five U.S. dollars.

Less than a minute later, Bud appeared near Danny silently, startling both Danny and Craig.

"You two seem very jumpy, even for Americans," Bud said.

"It's been a long few days," Danny said.

"How bad are these people you are hiding from?" Bud asked.

"Bad," Craig said and Danny nodded.

Bud frowned, then said, "The twins will talk with you if you bring us all some lunch." He pointed to a cart making some sort of wrap of meat and bread. "Five of those, five bottles of Coca-Cola."

"Heaven," Craig said, as all three headed toward the booth where a woman worked and two children sat in the shade on the ground behind her. The entire lunch cost Danny two pounds, including five warm small bottles of Coke, and the woman seemed very happy with that much.

As they walked away, Bud said in a disgusted voice, "You should have only given her one. You two Americans really do need my help."

Danny was starting to believe him.

The twins' apartment, as Bud had called it, was no more than a room not much larger than an average bedroom. It had two sleeping pads against the back walls, one window that was open, and one table with two chairs. If there was a bathroom, it was down the hall or outside.

The place actually felt slightly cooler than out on the street, but

Danny wasn't sure if that was because they were out of the sun or if it actually was cooler.

Bud had been right about the twins being Danny's age. They actually looked a little younger, with startling dark black skin, short-cropped hair, and smiles that seemed to light up the room.

They were clearly identical twins and Danny could see no difference at all, not even a mannerism that separated Ernie from Ed. Thankfully, Ernie had a small silver stud earring in his right ear, while Ed had the same earring in his left. Otherwise they were completely identical twins, so much so that they even finished each other's sentences and wore the same color brown robe.

Bud handed them the food and drink, and Ernie thanked Danny in a polite British accent.

No one sat at the table, since it was covered in papers and books, so all five of them ended up sitting on the floor with their backs against the bare, paint-peeling walls, eating.

Danny was stunned at how good the bread and meat tasted. Almost like a Sloppy Joe back home, only with a much sweeter spice and a very thin, dry bread. And he was so thirsty that even the warm Coke tasted great.

Danny thought he ate the food fast, but when he finished and looked up, Ernie, Ed, and Bud were sitting watching him, clearly waiting. Craig was still eating.

Ed looked at Danny, then at Craig. "We thought all young Americans your age were killing women and children in Vietnam."

Danny was stunned at the directness. He had spent the last few years worrying about being drafted and going to Vietnam. He hadn't realized that the rest of the world paid attention as well.

"College deferments," Craig said, staring back at Ed.

"I must apologize for my brother," Ernie said. "We just do not believe in what your country is doing."

"Half of our country doesn't either," Danny said. "It's why our cities and college campuses are being destroyed by bombs and people are marching in the streets."

Ed nodded. "I am sorry."

"Not a problem," Danny said, waving it off.

"So, what can we do to help you?" Ernie asked.

Danny didn't know where to start, so he figured a little background might ease him into what they needed. He introduced himself and Craig, using first names only, and told them where they were from in general.

"My father is an archeologist. He went missing a few weeks back and we're here looking for him."

"Professor Kenneth Hawk?" Ernie asked, suddenly sitting forward, clearly excited and very interested.

"You're his son?" Ed asked, also excited.

"You have his notebooks, don't you?" Ernie asked.

"And you need help reading them," Ed said. "Oh, this is so amazing."

Bud stared at the twins, then at Danny.

Danny didn't know what to say. Or do for that matter. He just sat there stunned.

Beside him, Craig's mouth was open.

"We would be honored to help you find your father," Ernie said.

Ed nodded. "Very honored. I hope my rude comment about your country's stupid war did not upset you too much. We have already been doing what we can to find your father."

"Without success," Ernie said.

"Sadly," Ed said.

"Yes, your father was a brilliant scientist and archeologist," Ernie said.

"He was onto something very large when he was taken," Ed said.

"Very large. Very important," Ernie said.

Danny held up his hand and stopped the constant talk of the twins. He was suddenly very worried that they had come to the wrong place. "How did you know my father?"

"We met him many times, and worked with him some on his latest dig," Ernie said.

"Only as brushers," Ed said.

"And dirt haulers," Ernie said.

"But we were still honored," Ed said.

Ernie only nodded in agreement.

"Oh, I knew these two could help you," Bud said, smiling. "I'm so good."

Danny glanced at Craig, then back at the twins, trying to clear his head. Finally he managed in the silence of the room to get back to what they had come here for. "Can you read Latin, Italian, or hieroglyphs?"

"Yes," both twins said at once.

Danny glanced at Craig, who was nodding. "Might as well tell them everything."

Danny shrugged. He had no choice. He was going to have to trust some people. Not everyone could be on the other side. His uncle wasn't even a few hours away from Egypt and they were making better progress in getting help than Danny could have hoped for in weeks. Assuming these two were not members of the Hydra League.

"My uncle Steve, Craig, and I arrived in Cairo two days ago," Danny said, "to start a search for my father, since the authorities and U.S. Embassy seem to have had no luck."

"They wouldn't either," Bud said. "Not with everything that's going on with the new government."

"And your father was taken by forces far more powerful and older than any government," Ernie said.

Ed nodded.

Danny didn't like the sound of that at all, but he went on. "Professor Davis at the American University had been given my father's notebooks to keep, since clearly my father was worried something would happen to him."

Ernie and Ed both nodded. "Yes, Professor Davis, a good man."

Danny took a deep breath. "I was in his back office when two men burst in and threatened him to get the notebooks. I ended up hiding on the ledge outside his back office window and they didn't see me."

"Oh, no," Ernie said.

"Professor Davis refused to tell them that he even knew what they were talking about," Danny said, going on. "So they killed him and searched his office. Then they cleaned up his office and took his body away, saying they would dump it in the desert."

Now it was Ernie and Ed's turn to look shocked. And Bud didn't look very happy now about even being with them.

"I also overheard them say that they would come looking for my uncle, Craig, and me, since we had just arrived and must have the notebooks."

"That's who you were afraid of following you in the bazaar?" Bud asked.

Danny nodded. "We managed to escape without them seeing us and found another hotel where we registered under false names. Then we bought three tickets back home to lead them in the wrong direction, but only my uncle used his ticket to go home and get my mother to safety. We stayed to continue the search."

"Very smart thinking," Ernie said.

"Yes, very," Ed said.

"So these killers may not know you are even still in Cairo," Bud said.

"That's what we're hoping," Craig said.

"So, you don't have your father's notebooks?" Ernie asked.

"No, I have them," Danny said. "They are very safely hidden. But we could only read a part of them, since my father alternated between English, Latin, Italian, and hieroglyphs."

"Do you have training in archaeology?" Ernie asked.

"Some," Danny said, "but not officially. Just from being around my father growing up, and listening to his stories when he came home."

"So," said Ed, "even if you could read it all, you might not understand it."

Danny nodded. He had considered that as well.

"So what was your father looking for that got him kidnapped and this Professor Davis killed?" Bud asked.

"The Fountain of Youth," Danny said.

Bud laughed, but Ernie and Ed both nodded.

"It is very real, and has been known about for centuries," Ernie said. "Your father had become the leading expert on it."

"But it is not a fountain," Ed said, just as seriously as Ernie. "Your father, of course, knew that."

"Actually, no one knows exactly what it is," Ernie said.

"But it is the world's most protected secret coming down through the centuries," Ed said.

"It is believed that many people have lived thousands of years because of what is called the Fountain," Ernie said.

"Who protects it?" Danny asked, worried that he already knew the answer. "Men in red hoods?"

Ernie and Ed looked stunned, but slowly both nodded.

"The Hydra League," they said together.

Craig shook his head and stared at the floor. "We are so screwed."

9

August 19, 1970
An apartment near the Khan Al-Khalili bazaar, Cairo, Egypt

They talked for another hour or so, and the more they talked, the more Danny came to trust all three of their new friends. He learned that the Hydra Journals his father was searching for weren't really journals in a traditional sense, but a series of clues that when put together would lead to the secret of the Fountain.

The Hydra League had supposedly been formed six centuries ago to protect the secret, and the journals' clues had been placed in various places around the globe. Taccola searched for one of them, as did Napoleon and his people.

"Both are said to have found one part of the Hydra Journals," Ed said.

"Do you think my father was close to finding another piece?" Danny asked.

The twins shrugged. "There was a reason he was taken. It was rumored he found the key to finding them all."

"So he's been killed," Danny said, very much afraid of the answer the twins might give him.

"I don't think so," Ed said.

"I think he was taken to the Fountain," Ernie said, and Ed nodded.

"What?" Danny said, surprised. "Why would a group that killed Professor Davis spare my father?"

"Even the Hydra League is rumored to have rules," Ed said. "Very old rules."

"You father cracked their secret code, we're sure," Ernie said. "And thus he would have earned the right to go to the Fountain, the world's greatest archeological treasure."

"But he's being held?"

"Of course," Ed said. "How else would the Hydra League protect its secret?"

"Sure," Ernie said. "They would only have to hold him for a hundred years or so. All of his family and friends would be dead, and who would he tell? And if he tried, who would believe him then?"

Danny felt all the energy drain out of his body. If these two were right, the chances of seeing his father again didn't exist.

"So, we crack the Hydra Journals and go rescue him," Craig said.

"Oh, sure, nothing to it," Bud said. Then he seemed to realize something and brightened. "If we did find this Fountain, it would be worth a great deal of money, wouldn't it? Count me in."

Ernie and Ed both shook their heads with looks of identical disgust.

Danny closed his eyes and leaned back, banging his head slightly on the wall. His father's only hope was him and these guys with him in this tiny Cairo apartment. But at least, as long as they were still alive and looking, trying to find him, there was still hope. No one else was going to go looking for his father, that was for sure.

The image of his father, tall, lean, hungry eyes, boarding the plane for Egypt the last time came to Danny's mind. His work had always consumed him, often more than his family. And Danny had always thought it somewhat stupid, digging in the ground for old things to put in museums.

But it seemed that the past held secrets that were deadly even to the present, and those secrets could change the world if they were exposed. Maybe it was time to tell the world that the Fountain of Youth was real.

The only chance of ever seeing his father again was to find the Fountain. They all needed to pick up the quest where his father had left off. And somehow not get taken by the Hydra League.

He had to actually follow the Hydra Journals, find all of its clues, and go to the Fountain and rescue his father. More than likely the quest would kill him, but he had no choice.

He had to try to save his father.

Danny sat forward and opened his eyes. "Ed, Ernie, would you help Craig and me search for my father?"

"Of course," both said at the same time.

"I will pay all expenses," Danny said, "including food and travel if we have to change cities."

Both nodded in agreement to the terms.

"And if we do find treasure, we divide the value evenly."

"I agree," Ed said, "but I would argue for the archeological treasure we might find be sold to museums."

"Of course," Danny said.

"Then I agree as well," Ernie said.

"How about a five-way split?" Bud asked. "You're going to need someone like me along on this adventure. I know how to find things. I got you four together, didn't I?"

Danny smiled at the short guy. "I was hoping you would want to join us. You're right, we are going to need you."

"You know," Craig said, "we all may get killed going after this."

"It's highly likely," Ernie said.

"But it is a great treasure," Ed said. "And great treasures are worth great risk. Danny, your father believed as much."

"I like that part," Bud said. "Great treasure."

Danny looked at them. "I have no choice. My father needs me. I'm his only hope."

Then he smiled. "But finding the Fountain of Youth wouldn't be all that bad either."

10

August 19, 1970
Gizera Hotel, Cairo, Egypt

The sun was dropping over the desert to the west when they finally left the twins' apartment. The bazaar had wound down in the heat of the day, and now the street looked almost deserted.

Waves of shimmering heat came off the pavement and Danny, this time with Bud's help, bought them all bottles of Coke again. Bud paid less than a quarter of a pound for the five bottles, and seemed upset that he hadn't gotten a better deal.

The five took two cabs to the hotel where Danny and Craig were staying. The twins and Bud took a cab to the hotel first, to scout out the area to make sure no one was waiting for Craig and Danny, who followed in a second cab a few minutes later.

There was no one, Bud swore to that, but Danny was convinced that their luck wouldn't last. He and Craig had to move to a safer place near the bazaar that couldn't be traced. Bud said he knew the best place, but he wouldn't be able to get it for them until tomorrow morning. So they decided to risk one more night in the hotel and all read Danny's father's journals while there.

Danny brought them all food after getting the notebooks from the hiding place in the ceiling tile. The twins were well into the notebooks, writing like crazy. They had brought second spiral notebooks, and were going to copy by hand every word Danny's father had said.

And put it all in English.

"Your father is an amazing man," Ernie said as he ate and read at the same time. "He put together clues from diverse sources that no other archeologist would have thought of doing."

"Yeah," Danny said, "but he wasn't much of a father."

"Never home?" Ed asked.

Danny nodded.

Bud shrugged. "Never knew my father. Or my mother for that matter."

Danny glanced at Bud. He had said it so matter-of-factly, it seemed like he actually didn't care. But Danny had a hunch that under that tough shell, Bud actually did care.

"Our father was killed in prison for speaking out against the South African white government," Ed said.

"Our mother never recovered," Ernie said. "She was also killed for the same cause."

Bud glanced up at them, surprised. Clearly they were not runaways as he had suspected, except maybe running away from their country.

"My father drinks, can't hold a job, and gets mean," Craig said. "I try not to be around him much, but I still like the old guy."

Danny looked at his new friends, suddenly understanding just how lucky he had been to have the father he had. His mother had never complained, and neither had Uncle Steve. They had just accepted Professor Kenneth Hawk for what he was, a driven scientist in search of something mythical.

Danny had been the only one angry at him for not being home more. And now it was up to Danny to save his father.

After they finished eating, all five boys went back to reading, with Bud going out to check the surrounding area around the hotel every fifteen minutes.

Craig dozed off around one, and Danny finally fell asleep at two.

When he woke to the sun streaming in through the window, the two twins were still writing as fast as they could, and Bud was napping in a chair near the door.

"We almost have it finished," Ernie said without slowing down.

"Another fifteen minutes at most," Ed said.

"But I can tell you this much," Ernie said. "We're going to have to go to your father's apartment here in Cairo."

"Why?" Danny asked.

"We're not sure, but we need to go there."

Danny shrugged. More than likely it had been cleaned out, but if the twins thought it was a good idea to go there, they would do it.

"And we need to go to the Giza Pyramids," Ernie said.

"So you can see something your father found and understood," Ed said.

"Was my father's last work site there?"

"No," Ed said. "His dig was farther to the south."

Now Danny was really puzzled. "Why go to Giza then?"

"A clue to the Hydra Journals is there," Ed said. "We think you should see it."

"Wouldn't my father have taken it with him, or the Hydra League hidden it after they took him?"

"No," Ernie said, pointing to a place in the notebook that was written in hieroglyphs. "Because it's been in plain sight for years. Every tourist looks at it without understanding what it is. Your father finally put meaning behind what everyone sees."

"Oh," was all Danny could say.

The twins both went back to writing at full speed, so Danny decided he would get them all some breakfast.

"We're not going to either of those places without me checking out the area first," Bud said before Danny could stand. "And right now, I need to scout this hotel again. No one leave until I get back."

Bud moved quickly and went out the door, closing it carefully behind him.

Danny stayed in the chair he had been sleeping in and watched the twins work. He was very glad they had suggested making a copy of the notebooks and hiding both. That way, if the League did catch up to Danny, he could surrender the originals and still have what they needed to start their journey toward the Fountain and his father.

"Done," Ernie said.

"As am I," Ed said a moment later.

They quickly wrapped the original notebooks and put them back in their pack. Then they quickly took the four notebooks they had written in and hid them under their robes, in pockets that didn't seem to show the books at all.

"We have company," Bud said, coming back in quickly and closing the door.

"These guys are good," Craig said, sitting up and rubbing sleep out of his eyes. "Only two days to find us here."

The sound of the shot killing Professor Davis came back clearly in Danny's mind, but he pushed it away. "How many and where?"

"Only two, and they are at the front desk," Bud said. "But they have a picture of you, Danny, and the front desk clerk is chattering like a bird at sunrise."

"You three go out the window," Danny said, handing Bud a fifty-pound note. "Circle around to the front and take a cab back to the bazaar and wait for us. They don't know you, so you'll be safe."

Danny grabbed his bag and then put his father's backpack over his shoulder.

Craig grabbed his suitcase.

"How are you two getting out of here?" Bud asked, a worried look on his face.

"Right through the front lobby," Danny said. "We're even going to check out and everything, then head for the airport."

Bud smiled. "I'm starting to like you two more and more. You have some courage."

"That is taking a great risk," Ernie said.

"They know what we look like already," Danny said as he opened the window to hold it for the three new friends. "They won't dare confront us in a public place. We'll try to lose them at the airport, but if we don't we're going to need cover when we reach the bazaar."

"You'll have it," Bud said, going out the window right behind Edward.

"Good luck," Ernie said and ducked out as well.

"We're going to need it," Craig said as Danny closed and locked the window, then turned and headed for the door, glancing around the room as he went to make sure that they hadn't missed anything.

Danny was happy that at least now copies of his father's notebooks were in the hands of two twins who would never be suspected of having them.

Danny knew his plan of escape rested on the two men staying in the lobby or outside waiting and not trying anything until they had privacy and red hoods, as they had done with Professor Davis. It was a gamble, he knew that.

And he was betting his and Craig's life that he was right.

11

August 20, 1970
Cairo, Egypt

The hallway was thankfully empty, so Danny led the way down the hall toward the front desk. The restaurant was on the right of the big lobby. There were plants, small palm trees, and a dozen places to sit.

The two men that Bud had described were still standing at the front desk. Both were white. One looked British and very properly dressed in an expensive black suit. The other was of what looked like Italian descent, with big arms and a black suit that was two sizes too small. He looked mean, and his face had a nasty scar on the right cheek.

Clearly, the British-looking man was in charge. As Danny got closer to them, he could see that their skin had a weathered look to it all over. Not scarred, just weathered.

Danny had no idea if that was the same two who had killed Professor Davis, but if they were asking about him, he had no doubt they were with the same group.

"Remember," Danny whispered to Craig, "don't look at them. We don't know them. We're just checking out and heading home."

"You're nuts, you know that?" Craig whispered back as they crossed the open tile of the lobby and walked up behind the two men.

"Ah, Mr. Hawk," the desk clerk said loudly, looking over one man's shoulder.

Both men seemed to jump just slightly. Then one of them said to the clerk, "Thank you for the information. Please keep this to yourself."

"I understand," the clerk said, giving the man a sickly smile in return.

Danny wanted to just cut and run. He knew that voice. It was the man who had been in charge in Professor Davis's office, the man who had ordered the other to shoot the professor.

As the two men stepped off to one side, stopping close enough so that they could hear, Danny nodded to the clerk and gave him their room key.

"Checking out, going home," Danny said, pretending to be in a good mood.

"So soon?" the clerk asked, his voice trembling slightly. Clearly the two men had threatened him in some fashion or another.

"We've got to get ready for school," Danny said, trying his best to sound calm and relaxed, even though his heart was about to pound a new path right out of his chest. "It starts for us at the end of the month."

Craig stood beside him, pretending to read some sort of flyer that was on the counter. He had his back to the two men which, considering Craig's lack of a poker face, was a good thing.

"Where's your uncle?" the clerk asked as he wrote up Danny's receipt for the room.

"He left early yesterday," Danny said. "My mom needed his help. We wanted to stay and see the pyramids and everything yesterday, so he let us. Plus, we got my father's notebooks, which is what we came here to get."

He made sure his voice was loud enough that the men could hear him, and then to make it really clear, he patted the backpack he had on his shoulder.

Craig coughed and pretended to keep reading.

"Your father?" the clerk asked.

"Yes, he was an archeologist. These are his notes that I hope will help lead to where he is, but I can't read them. They're all Italian, Latin, and hieroglyphs. I figured someone back home can help me figure out what they say."

Craig coughed again and kept reading. Clearly Danny's little play was giving him a near heart attack.

"Well," the clerk said, glancing at the men, "have a good flight home."

Danny pocketed the receipt the clerk had given him and picked up his suitcase. "We will. Great food on the planes these days."

With that, he and Craig walked right past the two men who had killed Professor Davis.

Right past two members of the Hydra League.

Outside, in front of the door, was a cab that wasn't at the taxi stand twenty paces away. It had pulled up near the front door and had its back door open.

Bud must have set that up for them.

"Airport," Danny said as he started to climb in. A cab a few feet behind them honked long and loud, like a warning.

Danny suddenly realized that maybe Bud *hadn't* set up the taxi. Maybe it was the men inside, and the cab driver worked for them.

Danny quickly backed out, bumping into Craig and pushing him away. "Never mind," he said to the driver as he slammed the door.

The cab driver glanced back at Danny with an almost angry look on his face. Danny had a hunch they might have just escaped once again.

The two men came out the front door and watched as Danny and Craig moved toward the three cabs at the taxi stand.

Sitting behind the wheel of the second cab was Bud, smiling, a taxi driver's cap pulled down low over his head.

"Second cab," Danny whispered to Craig in case he hadn't seen Bud.

They quickly piled in the back seat, luggage and all, and before the door was even closed, Bud had the cab headed out of the cab line and toward the highway.

Danny glanced back as the two men got into the cab in front of the door and started to follow.

"Okay," Craig said to Bud, laughing, "how did you get this cab?"

"Driver had to use the bathroom and he got a little *tied* up," Bud said, shrugging as he focused on driving. "So I just thought we'd borrow it. We'll leave it at the airport, blocking traffic, of course. The twins took another cab and they will be waiting for us at the bazaar."

"The two men are in the cab behind us," Danny said, glancing back as if he were looking at the sights, not at the cab following them. His heart was still racing, and even though it was cool in the early morning hours, he was sweating.

"I know," Bud said. "Don't worry, we'll lose them in traffic or at the airport."

"You had me scared to death with that act at the front desk," Craig said, sitting back and shaking his head at Danny. "I thought they would just step up and grab the journals right there."

"I knew they wouldn't, once I had them convinced we didn't know they were following us. They'll wait for the right time."

"Was it the men in Professor Davis's office?" Bud asked.

"It was," Danny said, trying not to shudder. "I recognized one of their voices."

"They are mean-looking, that's for sure," Craig said. "Cold eyes."

"Very cold," Danny said, forcing himself to breathe evenly. It was one thing to talk about going after his father and risking his life, but it was clearly another matter to actually be in danger.

"And nice job telling them we hadn't read the journals yet," Craig said.

"You did?" Bud asked, glancing back with a smile. "Nifty trick."

"You think that might save our lives when they do catch up with us?" Craig asked.

"Probably not," Danny said, sinking into the seat. "But it was worth the try just in case."

12

August 20, 1970
Cairo, Egypt

Bud, even though he was barely tall enough to see over the dashboard, wound the cab through the thick Cairo traffic like a racecar driver trying to gain the lead.

As Danny watched, the cab with the two Hydra League killers behind them was cut off time after time, falling farther and farther behind in the thick traffic as they got closer to the airport.

Finally, they were so far back, Danny wasn't even sure which cab they were in in the sea of black and white cabs heading for the International Airport.

"When I pull up at the terminal," Bud said, "open both doors, then close them and duck down so you can't be seen. And stay down until I say otherwise, even if we're moving."

"Got it," Danny said. He was trusting Bud completely with his life at this point.

Danny tossed his suitcase over the seat and onto the front seat floor as Craig crammed his suitcase down onto the floor.

"Okay, get ready," Bud said.

He swung across two lanes and into a spot against the curb just in front of a small van. The sidewalk was crowded with passengers and their luggage going into the international terminal.

Craig opened the side door and Danny opened the door on the road side.

Then they both slammed them closed and ducked down onto the floor, trying to get as low as they could. The backseat of the taxi was cramped, but unless someone looked in, Danny was sure no one passing by in another cab would be able to see them.

"They're going past us," Bud whispered, sitting up on his legs so that he looked taller than he really was.

The seconds seemed to tick past as Danny held himself in the cramped position tucked down low.

"I'm going to ache in the morning from this," Craig whispered.

"Better than being dead in the morning," Bud whispered back.

"They have seen me," Bud whispered, pretending to count cash. "The cab is pulling in three cars ahead of us and the two men are getting out. Stay down."

Bud suddenly pulled the cab back out into traffic and moved over two lanes.

"The two men are going into the terminal," Bud whispered. "And the other cab is waiting for them. Stay down a little longer, until we get out of sight completely."

The cab bumped and jerked, and in the position Danny was, crammed on the floor of the back seat, his head down against his knees, he had no doubt that Craig was right, they were going to be very sore from this in the morning. And bruised from every bump that Bud hit.

The cab jerked right, then picked up speed.

"Clear," Bud said.

Danny tried to stretch his cramped muscles as he climbed back onto the seat.

"Great work," Danny said to Bud, reaching forward and patting him on the shoulder. "I'm really glad you're with us."

"Yeah, me too," Craig said.

Bud laughed. "Makes the days interesting."

"What, trying to stay alive?" Craig asked, laughing.

"I've been doing that for five years," Bud said. "But I will admit, this is new."

"Next stop, while we have them busy searching the airport, is my father's apartment," Danny said. "We need to know if the twins are right in there being something in the apartment that we need to see."

"Address?" Bud asked, like a regular driver would do.

Danny gave it to him, then sat back and tried to once again get his heart to calm down and stop racing. He really wished he had spent more time in training with his grandfather. Staying calm would come in really handy right about now.

13

August 20, 1970
Cairo, Egypt

Bud drove past the small apartment building twice before finally backing the cab into a hidden driveway and stopping in the shade.

The neighborhood around the two-story apartment building looked to be an older residential one, with small buildings packed in tight together. No lawns or shrubs like in the States, just rocks and peeling paint. Some of the houses had laundry hanging in the front or side yards. It was far too hot for anyone to be outside in the sun, so everything felt abandoned.

"I'll keep the car running and if you hear a honk, come running. It will be hard to escape this neighborhood."

"Got it," Danny said. "We won't be long."

"So, what's the plan?" Craig asked as they climbed up the exposed outside stairs to the second floor and faced the wooden door.

Danny dug for the key in his pocket that his mother had given him.

His father had sent it to her as a backup, in case something happened to him and she needed to come here. He always kept the rent paid up for months in advance so nothing would be disturbed by the landlord at least.

"We gather up what we think might be important, then get out of here," Danny said. "We'll let the twins figure out if what we got is important or not."

"As good a plan as any," Craig said.

"No talking inside," Danny said. "It might be bugged."

Craig nodded. "Good thinking. I've just got to get more paranoid."

Danny unlocked the door and slowly pushed it open.

There were no lights, so he stepped inside and let Craig follow before shutting the door and flipping on a light switch.

The place smelled musty and unused. At least it was much cooler than outside.

The living and dining areas were almost empty. A wooden table with two metal folding chairs were in the dining room, and a couch that had clearly seen far too much use was the only thing in the living room.

Danny glanced at Craig who was shaking his head at what greeted them.

The tiny kitchen had a few glasses and chipped bowls in one cupboard and that was it. Not even a dirty dish in the sink.

Everything had been cleaned off and wiped down. Danny knew his father was known for being a slob. His mother complained about it all the time, sometimes even going so far as wishing he would leave on another dig so that the house would be clean again.

Danny knew that his father put all his attention into his work. Keeping a clean apartment was just an annoyance left up to others.

If Danny's father had lived here, someone had gone to a lot of trouble to make sure nothing was left of how he lived.

Or any of his personal things.

The one bedroom had a made bed against one wall and a small

wooden desk against a second wall. The desk was empty. As was the closet and bathroom. The bed was made like a maid had done it.

Danny wasn't really that surprised. At least not as surprised as he would have been if he had come here first from the airport three days ago. Someone clearly had come in and taken all of his father's things and cleaned the place. The only thing left was a large world map that somehow his father had glued like wallpaper to the wall.

Craig pointed to it after Danny finished checking every corner of the closet.

Danny stepped over to the map. Small "x-marks" had been made in blue ink, at least a dozen of them all over the world.

South America's western coast area had two. One over New York City, three over London and the surrounding area. Another in the Soviet Union behind the Iron Curtain. Even more in Egypt, China, Mongolia, and India.

Danny studied the marks, not having a clue what they had meant to his father. But his father had put those marks on that map for a reason, Danny was sure of that.

Danny tried to pry the map off, but it was glued completely. It would completely destroy the map and the wall to take it off.

The only reason he and Craig were seeing the map with the marks was because the map had been impossible to peel off and the people who had cleaned out the apartment had just left it.

Danny leaned over to Craig and whispered in his ear. "Memorize the exact locations of all the marks."

Craig nodded and both he and Danny stood in the nearly empty apartment for the next few minutes doing just that, like they were both studying for a geography test in school.

After Danny felt like he had the dozen or so marks clear in his mind, he motioned for Craig that they should get out of there.

He locked the door behind them and quickly went through the heat down the stairs to where Bud waited in the running cab.

Bud was clearly happy to see them. "Starting to worry me. Find anything."

"Place had been cleaned out," Craig said as Bud pulled out of the driveway and headed back into town.

"Except for a map glued to the wall with a bunch of marks on it," Danny said. "I just hope we can remember where all the marks were. We need to write them down later, while it is still fresh."

"Yeah," Craig said. "And better yet, at some point figure out what they mean."

Danny couldn't agree more.

"One more stop," Danny said. "But we have to pick up the twins before we go there."

"The Pyramids of Giza?" Craig asked.

Danny nodded.

"Well," Craig said, "at least I get to be a tourist before some goon kills me."

14

August 20, 1970
Giza Plateau, Egypt

One block away from the bazaar, Bud parked the cab in a shaded alley so narrow that Danny was amazed that Bud could get the cab backed in and still get the door open. Bud was small enough to squeeze out the door somehow and vanished around the corner, leaving Danny and Craig sitting in the cab, clearly trapped. They were both too big to even climb out the open windows between the car and the walls.

And on top of that, the alley smelled of urine and some sort of fried meat. The two odors did not combine well.

"You ever wonder what has just happened to our nice, normal lives?" Craig asked.

"Most of the last three days," Danny said. "So much for football practice starting next week."

"And the homecoming dance I suppose is now out of the question as well," Craig said, shaking his head. "I was really looking forward to maybe asking Karen. I would have loved dancing with her."

"Slow-dancing," Danny said, smiling at his best friend. "You fast-dance like a monkey."

"It's all the rage," Craig laughed. "Or haven't you heard?"

At that moment, Bud slid back into the car and pulled the car to the front of the alley where Ernie and Ed had room to climb in, Ernie in the front seat, Ed in the back beside Craig.

"Field trip," Craig said as Bud pulled out into the busy traffic, narrowly missing another cab and causing at least three cars to swerve to miss him.

"You have your translations in a safe place?" Danny asked, feeling the backpack on the floor beside his leg with his father's original notebooks.

"Hidden safe and sound," Ed said.

"Don't tell us where," Craig said, holding up his hand. "I think it's better that we just don't know."

Danny nodded.

Bud turned west and headed out a wide highway, picking up speed and making it impossible to talk with all four of the windows rolled down. He was going faster than Danny thought any street kid should be allowed to drive. And just like he had done on the main streets, Bud was swerving in and out of traffic.

Danny just held onto the door handle and let the wind blow in his face from the four open windows.

Ahead of them, the three larger pyramids of Giza seemed to grow like mountains as the road climbed out of the city and up to the sands of the desert. Actually, the pyramids were very close to the edge of the city. Danny had no doubt that in forty years, the city would surround the entire Giza Necropolis. From what he had heard, the smog was already starting to eat at them, and just recently, people had been barred from climbing on the pyramids anymore.

There was no way to describe the awe that Danny felt seeing those huge stone pyramids grow bigger and bigger in front of him. How could anyone have built them? Now he understood that age-old question. Pictures just didn't do them justice and there was nothing in the United States that even compared.

For a few miles, all of them just stared. Craig his mouth slightly open, just kept shaking his head, as if he wasn't believing what he was seeing. Danny understood that feeling.

The most famous of the pyramids was the Great Pyramid of Khufu, the second was the Pyramid of Khafre, and the smaller one, still a giant structure but dwarfed by the other two, was the Pyramid of Menkaure. There were a lot of other smaller pyramid-like structures scattered around the base of the big three. They were called The Queen's Pyramids by many.

Three smaller Queen's Pyramids were between Khufu and the Eastern Cemetery. The Western Cemetery was on the other side of Khufu, and three smaller still pyramids were lined up beside Menkaure.

The entire area was huge. But it was the three monster pyramids that dwarfed everything.

"So, where are we headed?" Bud shouted to Ed.

"The Great Sphinx," Ed shouted back over the winds.

Bud nodded and headed to the east to a parking lot there.

Danny wanted to ask him why the Sphinx, what his father had said in the notebooks that was taking them here, but decided to wait until they stopped so they could talk normally. The idea of rolling up the windows in this hot air was just an insane thought.

Finally, Bud pulled the cab into a place facing the Great Sphinx and shut off the engine. There were only two other cars in the parking area, and Danny could see no other people around at all. The stones and shallow valleys were such that hundreds of people could be in the area and not be seen from the parking lot.

The silence was like a thunderclap to Danny. He was startled by it, after being in the cab and in the city and the bazaar. Out here there was only the wind blowing over the sand and that seemed to suck away noise like a soundproof room.

They all piled out of the cab and headed up the tourist sidewalk.

The Great Pyramid towered over everything, a good fifty stories tall. Danny couldn't believe how large it was. He just kept staring up at it.

Finally, after a dozen steps in silence, Danny got his head together and asked the twins, "Where was my father's dig from here?"

"Abusir," Ed said.

"To the south and east of here about twelve kilometers," Ernie said, pointing up the Nile.

Ed nodded. "Your father believed that under the Fifth Dynasty cemeteries of Abusir were remains of a much older civilization, dating back to far before King Scorpion in what is called the Archaic Period."

"Far older than four thousand years B.C." Ernie said.

"That's old," Craig said, shaking his head.

"Isn't the Great Sphinx believed to be much older than the Fourth Dynasty pyramids built here?" Danny asked.

Both Ed and Ernie shook their heads no.

"It was built in the stone quarry for the Great Pyramid, by Khufu's men," Ed said.

"But," Ernie said, "the famous Hall of Records from the legendary civilization of Atlantis is supposed to be buried somewhere near the Great Sphinx."

"Edgar Cayce predicted that would be where it was found," Ed said.

"Your father believes it is here as well," Ernie said.

"Atlantis?" Craig asked.

Ed nodded. "It is believed to have existed before the great dynasties of Egypt, and the survivors from the great disaster flocked to the Nile valley and other places around the world to live and rebuild."

"The Hydra League was formed in the time of Atlantis," Ernie said.

Danny just shook his head and stared up at the ancient pyramids, amazed at what it must have taken four thousand years ago to build them. If he had been sitting at home, on his couch, he would have never believed any of what Ed and Ernie were telling him. But Danny had men from this Hydra League after him now, and he was facing giant pyramids that he doubted that 1970's technology could build. So he was willing to believe just about anything at the moment.

They moved past the Valley Temple and up a dirt walkway until suddenly the giant cat-like stone figure sort of appeared in front of them, towering over them with the Great Pyramid behind it.

"Oh, wow," Craig said, stopping and staring up at the towering carving. It was a man's head on a lion's body, with huge paws extending away from the body. Clearly the air and time had done a lot of damage to the Sphinx, since its nose and part of its face were missing. But it was still very, very impressive.

"Nose fell off about a thousand years ago," Ed said.

"Napoleon's artillerymen were rumored to have used the Sphinx for target practice as well," Ernie said. "When only its head was sticking out of the sand."

"But for most of its life, it was buried," Ed said. "The sand around its base, in fact, was just cleared away twenty years ago."

Danny's mind just didn't want to accept that the huge stone creature in front of him was even real. But yet it was.

For the first time, Danny was starting to understand his father's passion toward archeology. So many questions, so few answers.

15

August 20, 1970
Giza Plateau, Egypt

"I'm going to keep an eye out for our friends," Bud said. "You enjoy the tour."

The short kid turned and just silently vanished behind a huge stone before Danny could even agree that it was a good idea. He couldn't imagine how the men could follow them from the airport to here, but anything was possible. Better to have Bud watching their backs.

The twins led the way into what they called the Valley Temple, a series of tall blocks to the left and in front of the Sphinx.

Over what looked like a main entrance to the temple was a stone placed between two other stones. Carved into the stone were a series of hieroglyphs.

Ed pointed to them.

"What does it say?" Craig asked, staring up at the very old writings.

Danny had a hunch what it said because he could see a number of snakes seemingly flowing together.

"What many think it says is simply a blessing for those entering this temple built in the Fourth Dynasty," Ed said.

"But Danny," Ernie said, "your father believed it meant something else, and that the stone was put there to mark the entrance or the general location to the Hall of Records."

Ed nodded. "It says, basically, that knowledge is protected by many snakes and the ten great puzzles of life."

"Hydra League," Danny said softly.

"The term Hydra is commonly thought to have an ancient Greek origin," Ernie said. "But the idea of snakes was common along the Nile, and they were often worshipped or feared as evil spirits or powerful gods, depending on the time. So this is not out of place."

"Ten puzzles?" Craig asked.

"This saying," Ed said to Danny, "got your father started putting together what he believed were ten clues called the Hydra Journals."

"Clues," Ernie said, "actually riddles that would lead to the location of the Fountain of Youth. And from there, maybe even the exact location of the Hall of Records."

"The Hydra Journals are a series of riddles?" Craig asked. "Great. I hate riddles."

"These riddles are as old as time, and your father had found three of them," Ed said.

"We have company!" Bud said as he came running around a large stone and skidded to a halt in the sand. "The three guys in the cab from the hotel just pulled up out front and parked next to a tour bus and a few other cars that just arrived. I don't think they saw our car."

"How did they follow us to here?" Craig asked, looking stunned.

Danny felt just as stunned as Craig felt.

"They know the details of your father's work," Ed said.

"This would be a logical place to check out," Ernie said.

"That's right, they may not know we are here," Bud said. "They weren't acting like they did."

Ernie pointed up at the second pyramid, talking quickly to Bud. "The main road comes in on the north side of the Pyramid of Khafre. There is a side road that runs up near the Western Cemetery. Think you can get the cab without being seen and meet us there?"

"I can," Bud said, nodding and again vanishing between the large stones.

"We need to head to the north and into the cover of the Eastern Cemetery," Ernie said.

"Isn't there a causeway the Pharaohs built between here and the Pyramid of Khafre?" Danny asked, remembering some of his reading about these pyramids.

"There is," Ed said. "But it is too exposed and we would be seen easily."

Danny nodded. "Lead the way."

At full run, the boys headed out through the stones, staying as low as they could as they moved behind the Sphinx. There was on open stretch of sand between the back of the Great Sphinx and the first blocks and mounds and small pyramids of the Eastern Cemetery.

Just the run along the length of the Sphinx had Danny sweating and breathing hard. The heat was intense, and he had no doubt that he and Craig couldn't stay out in this very long.

Ernie motioned for them to stay in the slight shade of the back of the Sphinx and quickly climbed up its side, moving like he had done it a hundred times in his sandaled feet. Danny was impressed. Clearly the twins were a lot stronger and in much better shape than they looked.

And they were used to working in the intense heat of the desert.

Ernie found a spot where he must have been able to see back toward the temple and the parking lot. With one quick look, he came scrambling back down.

"The three men are going into the temple," Ernie said. "We have to run now!"

He led the way out into the sun and across the hot sand, with Craig right behind him and Danny following his best friend very closely. Ed seemed to almost be pushing Danny from behind, and clearly wasn't working as hard as Danny was.

Running in the sand was like a football coach's dream for how to torture his high school team. As sophomores, their football coach had had them run sand dunes for exercise one day. Danny had hated that, and he hated running in the sand now.

It seemed to take an eternity for them to reach the tall stone blocks of the cemetery. And when they finally did, Ernie didn't even slow down. He turned to the west, staying between the smaller pyramids and stone funeral structures of the cemetery. He led them toward the southern edge of the Great Pyramid.

Up close, Danny couldn't believe the size of the blocks that the pyramid was constructed out of. They were taller in places than he was. He couldn't believe people used to climb them for sport.

The four of them ran along the hardened tourist path that framed the south wall of the Great Pyramid, then on around to the west side. They ducked into the cover of the Western Cemetery, finally stopping in the shade near the north side of the Pyramid of Khafre.

Danny worked to catch his breath, and he could feel the heat making him light-headed.

"We're going to need water," Craig managed to choke out between sobbing breaths.

"Only if we live," Danny said, his throat feeling like sandpaper had been scraped along the inside of it.

Suddenly, in a cloud of dust and sand, a cab appeared, bouncing off the main road and fishtailing over the dirt toward where they were hidden. Behind the wheel, Bud grinned like a kid enjoying a new Christmas present.

They all piled in almost before Bud had slid the cab to a stop. A moment later, he was accelerating out of the western parking area, headed toward the main road.

Danny had climbed into the front seat this time, and he turned to Bud. "Did they see you leave?"

"Nope," he said. "They were up in the temple area and I doubt they even heard me start the cab."

Danny leaned his head out the window and let the hot wind cool him some. Was this going to be the rest of his life? Staying just a few steps ahead of sure death at the hands of the Hydra League?

He hoped not, but if that was what it was going to take to save his father, then so be it.

"Now," Bud said, shouting over the wind so everyone could hear, "anyone got a problem getting back to the bazaar? I have to get out of this cab before the police spot it. I have no desire to spend the next twenty years in jail while you four go on and find the treasure without me."

"We'd visit you," Craig said.

"Yeah," Danny said, taking a deep breath and trying to get himself to relax a little. "As long as we're alive."

16

August 20, 1970
Khan Al-Khalili bazaar, Cairo, Egypt.

Danny Hawk felt like he might end up with a sore neck at any moment because he was twisting around so much, looking at the crowds around him, like every man or woman could be after him.

And they just might be.

He kept waiting for a knife to be thrust into his stomach from a man walking past, or a gunshot to rock him backwards into a booth. His imagination was making everyone look like a Hydra League member out to kill him.

He stared at everyone's hands, looking for the tattoo of the snake's head rising out of a pool of water that indicated Hydra League membership. Or at least Danny thought it did. The two men who had killed the professor both had the tattoo.

And in the crowds of this bazaar, there were thousands and thousands of people crammed into the streets.

Thousands of possible enemies.

There was an old man sitting on an ancient WWII motorcycle. Could he be the enemy?

Or what about the sinister-looking jewelry vendor with the thick brows and a gold tooth?

Anyone could be the one who kills him and takes his father's notebooks.

Anyone.

That had Danny scared to death, gripping his backpack with a death grip that made his hand ache.

The narrow streets of the bazaar felt like it must have felt a few thousand years ago. The smells of rich food, new carpets, and incense filled the air like a thick shield. Everyone was dressed in the traditional loose Arab robes, and all the women had their heads covered. The street was so jammed with booths, small tents, and people that it was almost impossible to move anywhere.

Since Danny and his best friend, Craig, were Americans, still dressed in their jeans and light shirts, everyone in the bazaar looked at them with suspicion, while at the same time seeming to want to sell them something.

Danny kept a firm hand on his backpack, which held his clothes and his father's original journals, and checked it every time it got bumped.

After twenty halting paces into the crowd, Danny felt the tug of Bud's hand on his shirt. He was yanked hard down and to the right, close to a stone wall.

"Get down!" Bud shouted to the other three.

A moment later, a shot rang out over the bazaar and a bullet smashed into the wall near Ed Black, one of the twins, not more than ten feet from Danny.

The echo of the first shot sent the thousands of people in the bazaar into a panic. Everyone tried to get out of the way at the same time, all moving in different directions.

The sounds of the screams and shouting was deafening.

Chaos.

A second shot rang out. It hit the wall close to Danny, between him and the twins, and just above their heads.

"Too close!" Craig shouted from behind Danny.

People screaming and running smashed into Danny as he tried to stay down and against the wall. He got kicked hard twice, and had yet another man trip over him a moment later.

From what Danny could see, his four friends were taking the same punishment. He had no idea where the shots had come from, but they were clearly aimed at the five of them. And where they were crouched, they had no real cover.

"The shooter's on the far roof!" Bud shouted, pointing up through the swirling crowds at the other side of the bazaar. At that moment, another shot cut through the screams and shouting and a man fell just a few feet from Danny.

"Follow me!" Bud shouted and headed along the right side of the bazaar, staying low.

Bud was short, and he looked more like a bum because of the tattered clothes. But Danny already knew the clothes were just a disguise to make Bud not be noticed in his many scams and tricks on tourists. Bud had lived on these streets for years. He could move through the bazaar crowds like a ghost, and Danny was noticing that Bud never seemed to miss a detail. It was a special talent he had, and Danny was happy to have him helping them stay alive right now.

Staying low, below the level of the frightened crowds, Danny ran along the wall, following Bud.

Craig was right behind him, and the twins brought up the rear.

Another two shots sent stone chips flying from the wall near Danny.

Another man fell face first onto the street.

Danny had to get out of these crowds. Too many innocent people were getting hurt.

All this was because of the notebooks Danny carried on his back.

His father's notebooks.

They ran past booth after booth, staying low and against the stone walls of the buildings. There were no more shots. They must have outdistanced the shooter for the moment, but Danny had no doubt the man, or men, would be right behind them.

Two-story buildings blocked some of the mid-morning sunlight from reaching the street, and Bud stayed in the shadows, leading them at full run through the vendors.

Suddenly Bud turned into an alcove and went down a dark side alley. The intense sounds of panic in the bazaar were cut off by the narrow alley like someone had thrown a switch. It became only a background rumble, like waves on a distant beach.

At a fast run, they all went up a long, narrow staircase without handrails and turned left at the top toward the twins' apartment.

"Everyone all right?" Bud asked, stopping for a moment in the narrow hallway as Ernie Black pushed past and fumbled to open a door across from their apartment.

Danny nodded, trying to catch his breath as he glanced around at his friends. All of them looked like they had escaped the shooter, at least this time.

Next time, they might not all be so lucky.

"We also rent this apartment under another name," Ernie said, indicating a door he was fighting to open.

"I really don't think it's a good idea to stop here," Craig said, glancing back down at the staircase behind them.

"We're not," Bud said.

"I need to hide these," Danny said, patting his backpack and his father's original journals. The twins still carried the copies that they had translated last night in the hotel room. But the men chasing them were after the originals.

Ernie shoved the door open finally. Everyone crowded inside except Bud, who said, "I'm going to see how far behind that shooter is." He turned and headed back down the stairs toward the alley.

The room was tiny, the size of a small bedroom, and completely empty except for two chairs and a small wooden table with a scarred top. A window led out to a rooftop.

The twins' other apartment was across the hall.

"Why two apartments?" Danny asked, turning from the window. "One for each of you?"

Ernie shook his head. "Safety." He pointed to the window. "Another way of escape from this top floor. We're going out that way."

"Why?" Danny asked. "Something to do with what my father found?"

Ernie shook his head. "Our father."

"The South African government?" Craig asked before Danny could.

Ernie nodded. "They killed our mother trying to get to us. We were very vocal after they killed our father, and led demonstrations against them. We are criminals in our own country."

Danny was shocked. That was the exact reason he had sent his uncle home to protect his mother, in case the Hydra League would go after her to get to Danny and the notebooks.

"I'm afraid," Ed said, "that if we help you, we will all also be running from not only the ancient and powerful Hydra League, but the South African government."

Ernie nodded. "In fact, it may be some of their operatives shooting at us, not the Hydra League."

Danny didn't much like the sound of that, but at this point, he had no choice. He needed their help if he was to ever find his father. He smiled. "Well, at least that will make it interesting."

Danny just wished he felt as confident as he had tried to sound.

At that moment, Bud slammed into the apartment and quickly closed and locked the door.

"Three men in brown suits," he said breathlessly. "Headed up the stairs."

"Hydra?" Danny asked.

Bud shook his head. "I don't know. Couldn't see their hands. But I've never seen them before and they're all carrying big guns."

"Great," Craig said. "Now we have even more people out to kill us."

17

August 20, 1970
Near the Khan Al-Khalili bazaar, Cairo, Egypt

Bud ran to the window and pushed it up and open. "Let's go."

"We'll be right behind you," Ed said as he moved to one corner of the room and quickly pried up a loose floorboard. It didn't come easily, but it was clear Ed knew it would come.

"Put your father's journals in here," Ed said as Bud climbed out of the window and onto the roof. "We have paid for this apartment for a year. They will be safe."

Danny quickly took the notebooks out of the pack, knelt down, and shoved them between the floor joists, off to the right under a board still in place. If anyone did pry the board off, they would never see the notebooks.

Outside the door, the sounds of heavy footprints filled the hallway. It sounded like a herd of elephants had filled the building. Danny wasn't sure if the sound of his pounding heart was louder, though.

Ed quickly and silently replaced the board. It looked like it had never been removed. Danny knew that if something happened to the five of them, no one would ever find his father's work. It didn't seem like the right thing to do, but at this point, anyone who Danny might send those journals to would more than likely be killed. And Danny just couldn't put someone else at risk, no matter how much work his father had put into the research.

Ernie was half out the window, and Bud and Craig were already running across the rooftop.

"Hurry," Ed whispered to Danny.

With one last look at where he had hidden his father's life work, he ducked out the window and onto the hard, white sand of the flat rooftop. From here, he could see mostly roofs and walls of buildings. Laundry was hung in different places, blowing in the hot wind, and on another roof, a couple of children played a game in the shade.

Ed came out behind him and carefully closed the window. Then the two of them ran to follow the others. From inside the building, the sounds of someone banging on an apartment door could be heard even outside. Those men weren't going to be far behind, that was for sure.

"Run fast," Ed said breathlessly from behind Danny. "You have to jump."

Danny didn't have time to ask how far or when. He could see when.

Right in front of him Ernie, at full run, leaped into the air and disappeared downward over the edge of the building.

Danny wanted to ease up to the edge and look at what faced him, but instead he just kept running. If a fall killed him, so be it. More than likely it would be a quicker death than having the men behind him catch him.

He hit the edge of the roof in mid-stride and full running speed and jumped.

"Oh, nooooooo!" he shouted as he flew over the hard stone of a dark alley two stories below.

The distance across the alley to the next building, which was lower than the one they were on, was a good eight or nine feet.

He focused on it, willing himself to make it.

Everything seemed to move in slow motion as he sailed through the air, finally landing solidly on the other roof, stumbling, but still running.

Ed cleared the alley right behind him.

Ahead of them, Ernie turned and quickly started down a metal ladder attached to the side of the building. It led into yet another alley.

Danny got to the ladder as below Ernie reached the ground and then ducked inside a building. There was no sign of Bud or Craig.

Danny half climbed, half slid down the ladder, hitting the ground hard enough to jar his knees, but not hard enough to hurt himself.

The door led into a long, dark hallway that went through the middle of the entire building. On the other end, through a door, Bud was waiting like a doorman, holding open a cab door.

They had come out onto a main street of Cairo a few blocks to one side of the bazaar.

Danny piled into the back of the cab with Craig and Ernie.

A moment later, Ed jammed into the crowded back seat with them, then Bud slammed the door of the building closed and climbed into the front seat beside the driver.

Bud said something to the driver in Arabic that was clearly instructions. A moment later, the cab sped off, moving at full speed down the narrow side street and finally onto a wide boulevard.

All of them fought to catch their breath as the cab swerved through traffic, putting distance between them and the men with the guns.

Danny was sweating like he had never sweated before, and the hot wind coming through the open window didn't seem to help much.

They had escaped again.

For the moment.

Finally, Danny breathlessly asked Ernie, "Where are we going?"

"Your father's last dig," Ernie said. "You said you wanted to see it, remember?"

"Yeah," Danny said, sitting back in the seat and wishing his heart would stop racing. "But that was before people started shooting at us."

18

August 20, 1970
Cairo, Egypt

"Stop here," Bud shouted, pointing to a place beside a food cart on the sidewalk near the four-lane highway. The cab crossed two lanes and almost slid to a stop, half up on the sidewalk.

"What's wrong?" Craig asked, looking around, his blue eyes wide with worry. Before this trip to Egypt, Craig and Danny's biggest fear was making it to work and their college classes on time.

They were both in far, far over the heads.

Bud didn't say anything and motioned for them to stay in the cab.

Danny had no idea what the short Egyptian kid was up to.

Bud jumped out, talking quickly to the man in the food cart. A moment later, Bud started handing into the back seat what looked like wrapped meat sandwiches and warm bottles of Coca-Cola.

Food. Bud was getting them food.

It looked and smelled like heaven to Danny. He had forgotten they had skipped breakfast that morning and had had no time to eat in the bazaar. They needed food and drink, and Bud had been the only one to think of it.

It was like a fast pit-stop in a sports car race. Less than thirty seconds later, Bud was back in the cab and the cab was again speeding toward the western edge of town.

Bud said something to the cab driver in Arabic, then handed him a bottle of Coca-Cola.

The man seemed very happy to have it.

The wrapped meat tasted like a mild Sloppy Joe. And Danny had never thought a warm Coke could taste so good.

Danny ate, watched the neighborhoods of Cairo flash past, and thought about what he had read in his father's notebooks last night. Those notebooks were the key to all of them staying alive.

While reading them, it had become clear that over a decade ago, his father had decided to try to track down the historical background for the myth of the Fountain of Youth. From the dates in his journals, it had taken a few years for his father to get any traction at all on the goal.

Then the famous engineer Taccola came into the research about the time Danny would have been in his early teens. Taccola lived in Fifteenth Century Siena and was known for being ahead of his time in inventions concerning the movement of water. During the last of his life, Taccola had become focused on Egypt and had actually disappeared there in 1458.

In hieroglyphs, Danny's father had written a simple phrase that Taccola had found.

"Belief. The Water flows uphill."

His father had then later labeled that phrase "Hydra Journals Entry One."

Danny had no idea what that meant, and it seemed from what he read, neither did his father.

Napoleon was next in his father's research. It seemed that the French leader had been focused on discovering in Egypt a way to give his troops fantastic strength and long life. It seemed Napoleon didn't find what Taccola had found, but something different, which Danny's father had labeled "Hydra Journals Entry Two: The birth of a snake, the path of elephants."

His father had found reference to the Hydra League in some ancient texts and on stone hieroglyphs. As Danny read, it became clear that his father became more and more worried that the ancient organization still existed. And that he believed that some of the members might have been alive for far longer than humans normally lived.

By the end of his notes, it had become clear Danny's father believed the Hydra League did still exist, and its purpose was to only allow those worthy to find the Fountain of Youth.

He knew there were ten parts to the Hydra Journals, that must be followed to find eternal youth, and he again underlined the word "Map."

His father had then underlined another key phrase. "Fountain of Youth. Not Water. Something else."

His final entry in his notebooks was "Hydra Journals #3: Under the teeming masses, the river becomes clear, the path muddy."

Danny looked out at the buildings of Cairo flashing past. He had no idea what to do next. And he didn't even want to admit to himself how scared he was. He just kept those thoughts pushed back, out of the way, covered with the idea that he had no choice.

To find his father, he had to find the Fountain of Youth, and he had to find that Fountain by following a trail of ancient riddles.

He had never been much good at solving riddles. They just made him angry, and now his father was somewhere at the end of an ancient riddle, protected by men who thought nothing of killing innocent people to protect their secret.

Impossible.

Finally, with one last drink from his bottle of pop, Danny looked around at his friends crowded into the cab. "Do any of you have any idea what to do next, when we get to the dig?"

"We follow the clues," Ed said.

"That's our only logical path to the next clue," Ernie said, "and then the next."

Craig laughed. "Yeah, that's going to work."

"Belief: The water flows uphill," Bud said from the front seat, shaking his head. "What in the world does that mean?"

"You must put yourself in the shoes of ancients who lived six thousand years ago," Ernie said.

"The water flows uphill was a belief about the Nile in ancient times," Ed said. "And on a map with North up, the water of the Nile flows uphill as well."

"Wish I'd paid more attention in history class now," Craig said, shaking his head.

"But the Nile is a very long river," Danny said, at least glad that he now understood the first Hydra Journals Entry. The easy one. "How does that help us?"

"It doesn't," Ed said.

"Unless you have the second clue," Ernie said.

Bud shook his head. "The birth of a snake?"

"The headwaters of the Nile," Danny said, suddenly realizing what that phrase meant. "The Nile is a long snake on a map."

"Exactly," Ed said.

"And the path of elephants?" Craig asked.

Both twins just shrugged.

"So, we go to the headwaters of the Nile, find an elephant, and follow it," Bud said, shaking his head. "Where will that get us? And that third journal entry seems really crazy."

"That it does," Ernie said. "But if we go to the head of the snake, we may find something that will help us understand it."

"And maybe find the next riddle?" Bud asked.

Danny turned to the twins. "What are we going to see at my father's last dig?"

"Not much, to be honest," Ernie said. "More than likely, by this time, since it hasn't been protected, blowing sand has filled back in much of it."

Danny nodded. He had thought as much. "Then I don't need to see it. It might put us at risk again. They might be watching the site, assuming I would go there. We need to get out of this city. Let's find a way to get started up the Nile."

"Anything is better than hanging around here waiting to get shot," Craig said.

The twins nodded, so Bud turned to the driver and gave him new instructions in Arabic. A moment later, the cab was headed south, toward the edge of Cairo.

They rode in silence for a few minutes, then Craig laughed. "This has got to be the biggest wild-goose chase ever imagined. Actually, an ancient, deadly wild-riddle chase."

"True," Bud said, "but with a fantastic treasure at the end."

For Danny, the treasure at the end would be finding his father alive.

19

September 1, 1970
Upper Lake Nasser, Sudan

The first part of the trip up the Nile had been fantastic, at least from a tourist perspective.

They had somehow managed to get out of Cairo without being seen and book a boat going south up the river. They had slept the first night on the wood plank floor of one small cabin, taking turns because there was only room for three to sleep. For Danny, that felt better anyway, since the two who weren't sleeping stood guard.

At every major port, they got off the ship and hid, then changed ships and kept going, sometimes booking a nice tourist ship, other times catching rides on fishing boats.

With every face that looked their way, Danny imagined it might be one of the Hydra League.

Or one of the brown-shirted men who had chased them out of Ed and Ernie's apartment.

From Cairo, for the first 400 miles, between Abu Roash and El Kula, there seemed to be a mountain range of pyramids along the west bank. Many times, Danny wished he and the others were there to sightsee, but they weren't. Even the slightest halt at this point might be enough to get them killed.

When they had crossed out of Egypt and into Sudan on a ferry on the great Lake Nasser behind the Aswan Dam, they had been asked for their passports, but were paid no attention to after that.

Danny had been surprised that Bud even had a passport. Later, Bud told him he had found it in the street a few years back and just kept it. The kid's name on the passport was Anthony Penn, and it was British, which fit Bud's accent.

Both of the twins also had British passports, but Danny didn't want to ask them how they got those. He was just relieved to have no further trouble. It looked like they had made a clean escape.

But that night, as the ferry pulled into Wadi Halfa, Sudan, two men climbed on board. It was just after midnight, but the air was still hot. The night sky was full of stars, brighter than any night sky Danny could remember seeing.

Danny, who was standing guard at the time, knew at once that they had been found. It was the same two men who had killed Professor Davis back in Cairo. He would recognize those two men anywhere, especially with the distinctive snake-rising-out-of-water tattoo on their right hands.

Hydra League.

Danny wanted to be sick. They were six hundred miles up the Nile River, yet these two men had found them.

How was that possible?

"They found us," Danny whispered to the others, waking them. They were on the top deck of the three-level ferry, near the rear. "Hydra League men."

"How?" Craig asked, shocked. "Are they human?"

"I would not bet on it," Bud said.

Below, the two men split up, one going toward the bow, the other toward the stern.

Danny looked at the lit dock and the large Sudan village beyond. It seemed impossible to reach without being seen. The ferry was about to pull out, and clearly the two men planned on riding along. Once the ferry was into the middle of the huge Aswan Lake, the boys would have no chance of escape.

"We need to get down to the next level," Danny whispered.

"Then what?" Ernie asked, looking panicked in the faint light.

"We're trapped," Ed said.

"When the two come up the stairs to the second level," Danny said, "we go over the side to the first level. We'll have to be quick. We'll only have a few seconds."

"We'll need to wait there until just as the ferry is pulling out," Bud said, nodding. "Then make a jump for it."

"Exactly," Danny said, trying to breathe evenly to slow his heart from pounding right out of his chest.

They made a dash for the second deck, moving as silently as they all could on the wooden stairs. On the second level, Bud went on down the stairs to the first level to see where the men were while Danny, Craig, and the twins moved quickly to a place in the middle of the ship away from both staircases.

A moment later Bud came running back. "Get over the side," he said as he went past Danny and flipped himself over the railing, sliding down a support pole to the first deck.

All four of them followed Bud, with Danny going last. As he slid down, he caught a glimpse of one of the Hydra League killers coming up the stairs near the front of the ferry.

At that moment, a signal sounded, echoing through the night air. The ferry was going to pull out. The engines got louder and the ferry lurched into motion.

"We jump at the last minute," Danny said, running along the edge of the ferry's lowest deck. He got to a point near the stern, swung himself over the railing, his backpack on his shoulder, then waited for the dock to come sliding past.

The other four were in the same position beside him on the

outside of the rail. He would be the first to jump, and the dock looked like it was getting farther and farther away from the ferry.

He had to wait.

Time it right.

Too soon and he would hit the water, too late and he would do the same on the other side of the dock.

The ferry had really gained speed as he finally said, "Now!"

He jumped with all his strength.

The blackness of the water between the ferry and the dock seemed to be a vast expanse, but somehow, he cleared it, hitting the dock with a few running steps before stopping.

The others did the same. Craig, the last one off, actually hit and rolled, but came up all right.

On the boat, one of the men standing on the second deck yelled something in Arabic at them that Danny didn't completely understand, since most of it was swearing.

Danny waved at the man like he was a relative going on a cruise.

"Now, that's not nice," Craig said, laughing. "You really shouldn't tease the big man with a gun."

"True," Danny said, turning and heading for the city of Wadi Halfa as the ferry vanished into the darkness of the big lake. "But what's he going to do? Kill me twice?"

20

September 11, 1970
Upper Lake Nasser, Sudan

Danny figured the two men would circle back by land to the city to look for them, so they took another ferry an hour behind the last one and for the rest of the trip up the river didn't see anyone following them. It took another full week, making good speed, before they had reached Lake Albert. It wasn't the headwaters of the Nile exactly, but it was close. The river that led to Lake Victoria fed off of Lake Albert.

They stopped on the Republic of Congo side of the lake because of a conversation Ernie had had with a boat pilot a few hundred miles back. It seemed what was called "the path of elephants" by the natives was from the bank of Lake Albert, over a range of mountains and into the deep jungle of the Congo.

The elephants had been using the same path for thousands of years.

Danny had been stunned. There really was a "path of elephants."

"The area is haunted," Ernie had told them. "It's never really been explored. The pilot said it goes through what is called the Land of the Dead. None of the native tribes go near the area."

Bud had laughed. "Well, at least we won't have that problem. But we're going to need someone to guide us."

Ernie had nodded. "The captain gave me a name of a guide who would take us along the elephant path to the Land of the Dead."

In the small village of Bumia, ten miles inland along a mud road from the lake, they had found their guide, a skinny, older man with long grey hair and rotted teeth named Hassett.

At first, Danny wasn't sure the old man could help them, but then after watching him move around his hut-like home, it was clear the man was still in great physical shape.

Danny had told him what they wanted and his answer had been to laugh. When none of them laughed with him, he had asked simply. "Why would I take you five into the jungle?"

"I'm in search of my father," Danny said. "And our only clue is to walk the path of the elephants."

"Path of the elephants?" Hasset asked. "What do you know about that?"

"Nothing," Danny said. "That's why we want to hire you to walk it." Danny had made no mention of the Hydra League or anything else. Hassett had finally agreed and Bud had helped him with the negotiations for Hassett's fee and buying the supplies they would need.

Twenty-two days and nights of travel after leaving Cairo, they started off into the jungle.

In all his life, Danny had never been so scared. He was leading an expedition into an area of the world that had never been explored.

And he had no idea what he was looking for.

21

September 15, 1970
Deep in the jungle, Republic of Congo

Walking the path of the elephants had actually turned out to be fairly easy, considering the thick underbrush of the jungle that bordered the half-mile-wide band of brush and trees trampled down by the passage of thousands of elephants twice a year. Danny couldn't imagine even trying to walk through that jungle. It looked like a two-story green wall on both sides.

Except for watching for the mounds of what Craig called elephant chips, they made good time. And the dried elephant chips made great fuel for fires at night.

They never saw an elephant, either, but did see a few scattered remains of ones, rotting and smelling in the hot, humid air.

Hassett had warned them that if they felt the ground shaking, get off into the jungle fast. Elephants mostly moved along this path slowly, but at times they moved a lot faster, and then they were real dangerous.

At first, the bugs that seemed to be everywhere had driven them all crazy, but as Hassett had said would happen, they all got used to them, and from what Danny could tell, as soon as they did, the bugs seemed to almost stop bothering them.

After five days of hiking, mostly uphill toward what Hassett called Elephant Pass, Danny was getting frustrated. He and the others had no idea what they were looking for. The only clue was the words "teeming masses" in the Hydra Journals entry #3. And in this jungle, it sure didn't look like they would find any teeming masses of anything except insects.

"When do we enter the Land of the Dead?" Danny asked Hassett just after they started out on the fifth morning.

Hassett laughed, a sort of choking sound that Danny still wasn't used to. "Son, we've been in it for a day now."

"Can we stop and talk for a minute?" Danny asked.

Hassett shrugged and pointed to some shade to one side.

With the pack off his back, Danny told the twins that they were all in the Land of the Dead, and what Hassett had said.

"Are there any ruins in this area?" Ed asked Hassett.

"I wouldn't know," Hassett said. "Never been off this trail. Never had any reason to go bushwhacking out in that stuff." He pointed to the high wall of what looked to be solid green that bordered the path of elephants.

"Any high place we could look over the Land of the Dead area?" Ernie asked.

"Sure," Hassett said. "Later today we'll reach Elephant Pass. To the right there's Ishango Peak."

"Ishango?" both Ernie and Ed said at the same time.

Hassett nodded, surprised.

"Ishango is the name of an ancient people," Ernie said.

"Rumored to exist before the first Pharaohs," Ed said.

"Can you get us to that peak where we can look out over the Land of the Dead?" Danny asked Hassett.

"Sure," he said. "But before I do that, you are going to have to tell me the truth."

He looked around slowly at each of them, but no one said a word, so he kept going. "Two men have been following us for days, staying behind us, pacing us. What kind of trouble are you boys in?"

Danny thought his heart was going to stop. Craig dropped to the ground and just sat there shaking his head. Clearly, they had been found yet again.

Danny looked at Hassett, then at the twins, who both nodded that they should tell Hassett everything.

"How familiar are you with archeology?" Ed asked.

Hassett did his laugh, then said, "I have a degree in it from Oxford, back before any of you were born."

Now Danny was even more shocked.

Ed smiled. "You're Dr. Steven Hassett. Expert in pre-Egyptian empires. Discredited for your beliefs that at one time an advanced civilization had spread around the world on the equator."

Hassett bowed in acknowledgement.

Ed pointed at Danny. "We are looking for his father, Professor Kenneth Hawk. He was taken by the Hydra League."

Now it was Hassett's turn to be shocked. His face went white and he had to swallow before he spoke. "Ken was taken? Then he must have found the third Hydra Journals entry?"

"He did," Danny said, surprised that Hassett had known his father. "And I have his notebooks well hidden. We are after the fourth entry in the assumption that the only way to find my father is to follow the Hydra Journals."

"And that means those two men who have been following us are Hydra League," Hassett said, clearly suddenly very afraid. Now he too sat down, so Danny and the rest did as well.

"Have I said before how screwed we are?" Craig asked, shaking his head.

"I know these Hydra League men on sight," Danny said. "If you can take me back close enough so that I can see them, I will tell you for sure."

Hassett shook his head. "They have been pacing us very carefully.

They are not hunters, and are clearly out of their element here in the jungle. They are after you, and clearly hope you will lead them somewhere, and I will not take you to the old city if they are following."

"Old city?" both Ed and Ernie asked at the same time.

Hassett nodded. "Why do you think I've been living here, pretending to be a guide? This is called the Land of the Dead because of a city buried by the jungle centuries ago." He pointed to the right off the trail. "I have worked it, explored it, for twenty years now."

"We will give you the first three Hydra Journals entries if you take us to the city," Danny said.

Hassett stared at Danny for a moment, then nodded and stood. "I have the first two, but I need the third. You have a deal. But first we got to make sure we're not followed."

He turned and started up the path, moving at a good pace.

"Where are we going?" Danny asked, scrambling to get his pack on his back and follow.

"We're going to hide your friends," Hassett said. "then you and I are going to get rid of the men behind us."

22

September 15, 1970
Deep in the jungle, Republic of Congo

Hassett had Craig, the twins, and Bud hide in the jungle to the right of the path of elephants and warned them to not move for any reason, no matter what they heard or what happened. Then he used a branch to brush away their footprints where they had all entered the deep underbrush. Danny and Hassett also both left their packs, but Hassett kept a rifle he had been carrying over his shoulder.

"This way," Hassett said, turning and moving uphill through the jungle. Danny stayed with him for ten minutes, breathing hard and sweating even harder. Finally, Hassett held up his hand for Danny to be quiet, then moved to the edge of the jungle.

"Make no sudden movements," he whispered.

He then led Danny over a shallow rise along the edge of the jungle. It took a moment for Danny to realize what he was seeing. The half-mile-wide path had turned almost gray under the high trees ahead. Thousands and thousands of elephants were grazing and moving slowly down the hill.

"How did you know they were here?" Danny whispered.

Hassett pointed at the circling flocks of small birds. "They go where the elephants go."

The elephants' smell was thick in the air, like baskets of apples that had been left in the sun for days.

Danny had never seen an African elephant, and was stunned at their size, and of the size of the tusks the bulls had. He had heard that ivory poaching had been bad in some areas, but it didn't look like this massive herd had been found yet.

Danny stayed close to Hassett, moving as silently as he could as they worked their way past the elephants, past the lead bull who stood guard.

Hassett moved the two of them slightly out into the path above the elephants, then handed Danny some dry brush. "Get ready to wave this and run at them," Hassett said.

Danny finally understood what Hassett was planning.

Hassett grabbed another handful of long, dry grass, then took his rifle off his shoulder.

He lit Danny's brush with a pocket lighter, then his own, and said, "Now!"

Waving the burning grass in his hand, Danny ran at the herd of huge beasts, shouting as loud as he could.

Hassett did the same, firing his rifle into the air at the same time.

The noise and the sight of the flames spooked the herd almost instantly.

The bull trumpeted a warning, as did others, and almost as one, the entire herd turned and started down the path at a full run.

For a moment, all Danny could see was a massive wall of elephant butts disappearing into a cloud of dust.

Thousands of huge animals, all weighing thousands of pounds, all running at the same time. It was a sight that Danny had never imagined, or thought of ever seeing.

Danny dropped his torch and stamped it out.

Hassett did the same.

A couple of bull elephants trumpeted so loudly that Danny bet it could be heard miles below on Lake Albert.

The elephant stampede shook the ground like a strong earthquake, and the rumbling echoed over the jungle. The huge dust cloud drifted out over the jungle.

"How far will they run?" Danny shouted to Hassett over the intense noise.

"Far enough to take care of our friends and cover our tracks!" Hassett shouted back.

They stood and watched the amazing sight for a few moments, then Hassett led Danny back to the edge of the jungle. They plowed into the underbrush, staying in the deep jungle as they moved back down the hill toward Craig and the others.

He and Hassett joined up with Craig and the others, and with Hassett indicating they should be very quiet, he turned and led them deeper into the jungle, away from the path of elephants.

A very long, hot hour later of fighting their way down what seemed to be a narrow animal path, Danny finally asked Hassett, "When are we going to get to the lost city?"

Hassett laughed and kept going. "You've been in it for fifteen minutes."

That got all of them looking around, and now that Hassett had said that, Danny could see odd shapes buried by the dense growth of the jungle.

"How big was this place?" Craig asked, shouting his question over Danny's shoulder to Hassett.

Hassett entered a small meadow and stopped, dropping his pack in the shade under some large trees. "I figure that over a half million people lived here six or seven thousand years ago."

"Half million?" Danny said softly. He couldn't even imagine that, standing here in the jungle now. It would be like standing in downtown Los Angeles, after it was overgrown and all the tall buildings knocked down, and trying to imagine the size of the city.

"Welcome to the city of Ishango," Hassett said, waving his arm around in a wide circle.

He moved about twenty steps to one side of the meadow, beside what looked like a wall of vegetation and yanked on some growth, pulling aside the green to show stone blocks underneath.

Danny followed the angle of the green wall up through the trees, stunned as his mind tried to grasp what he was seeing.

"It's a temple," Ed said, his voice hushed.

"It seems we found our teeming masses," Craig said, shaking his head and looking around.

"Teeming masses?" Dr. Hassett asked.

Danny nodded. "Under the teeming masses, the river becomes clear, the path muddy."

"The third Hydra Journals entry?" Dr. Hassett asked.

Danny nodded. "It would seem that the teeming masses were the half million people who lived here."

"Well, I'll be," Hassett said, shaking his head and laughing. "I was so busy looking up, I never thought in twenty years to look down. I have no idea what's under this ancient city."

Danny had no doubt that to continue the search for his father, they needed to find out.

23

September 17, 1970
Lost City of Ishango, Deep in the jungle of the Republic of Congo

Two long days of searching later, Danny finally had some luck, but not the kind he had hoped for. The ground dropped away under him like an elevator suddenly falling.

Danny had been using a burning torch for light to explore a dark room in the back of the old temple while Craig went on down a narrow hallway. The thousands of years of jungle and hot weather had left nothing of the old city except the stones with which the Ishango people had built the city. If there had ever been wooden doors, they were long gone. And every stone structure was completely covered by jungle and shaded by tall trees. In the dark rooms inside the stone buildings, nothing lived except small animals and insects.

In two days, Danny had seen more large spiders than in a bad horror movie. So far, all of them had avoided the huge creatures hovering in webs in the dark rooms. The last thing any of them needed thousands of miles from any civilization and good doctors was to be bitten by a poisonous spider.

Or any other jungle creature for that matter.

As the floor dropped out from under him with a loud crack and Danny fell, he did two things, almost instinctively, and at the same time.

First, he shouted. "Craig!"

Second, as what he thought was a solid rock floor dropped away into blackness, he twisted around like a drill the coach had made them do in football practice last year. That way he was facing what he thought was the outside wall of the building.

He found himself falling through an open space filled with twisted roots.

He frantically grabbed for anything to slow his fall. Everything went into slow motion as he grabbed and ripped out handfuls of thin roots.

Finally, one of the roots held, but his grip didn't, and his momentum yanked his hand off the root as it swung him around.

But it slowed him enough to grab more roots, and they held, and after a moment, he found himself swinging in midair, close to what looked like a tall stone wall, holding on with all his might to handfuls of tree and plant roots.

His hands and shoulders hurt, but he was still alive.

Around him was complete darkness.

He couldn't even see his arms going past his face.

The air was cool and smelled of damp earth and mold. And there was a faint, distant sound of water running.

He forced himself to remain as still as he could and take deep breaths to let his pounding heart slow and his eyes adjust. It became clear that he wasn't in complete darkness, but close.

Carefully, he then looked down.

His torch had fallen all the way through the roots and somehow remained lit, showing faint outlines of the huge cavern-like room. He could see that he still had a good fifty feet to drop from where he was hanging.

His breath caught. Oh, wow, luckily, the roots had been here, like a false ceiling on the huge underground area, otherwise he would have been very dead on those rocks below.

Above him, the hole into the room he had been in was an impossible twenty feet over his head. And there was nothing to climb on. The layer of roots didn't extend all the way to the hole.

And besides that, he didn't trust himself to let go of the roots he was holding.

He forced himself to take yet another deep breath. His hands and shoulders were aching. He couldn't hold himself here for very long.

He twisted carefully around and searched for any kind of ledge on the rock wall near where he hung.

At first, he couldn't see anything, but then he spotted a crack between two stones where more roots were growing out into the open area just below him. The crack didn't look to be more than a few inches wide, but it was more than he had now, if he could get to it.

He got swinging gently, almost holding his breath for fear he would break or pull out the roots holding him.

Finally, he managed to get one foot on the ledge. It was more than a crack. It was actually a thin ledge about an inch wide.

He eased around and pressed his back against the cold wall, using the heels of his shoes to take the pressure off his arms.

The ledge felt solid under his feet, but after falling through the floor of that room, he wasn't trusting anything at this point. He still kept his tight grip on the roots that had saved him. But at least they weren't holding his entire weight anymore.

"Danny!"

Craig's voice echoed down to him from what seemed like an impossible distance away.

"Down here!" Danny shouted back. "But be careful. It's a long fall!"

The dark around him seemed to swallow Danny's voice. And it felt like something scampered across his feet on the ledge, but he ignored that. He didn't dare try to bend over. If he did, he would swing back out into space holding on to only the roots.

And he wasn't sure if he wanted to know what it was that lived in this dark cavern.

Above him, the light from Craig's torch outlined the hole where the rock floor Danny had been standing on had slipped away. Then Craig poked his head over the edge.

"Danny!" Craig shouted. Danny had no doubt that all Craig could see was his torch seventy feet below him on the rocks.

"About twenty feet below you," Danny said. "Stuck like Spider-Man on the wall."

"Oh, man, are you all right?" Craig asked, finally seeing Danny. "And how did you get there?"

"Just luck," Danny said. "But I think I found how to get under the old city."

"Yeah, I'd say," Craig said. "Can you hang on there? I'll go get the others and some rope. Actually, a lot of rope."

"I'm not going anywhere," Danny said. "But hurry, would you?"

"Right back," Craig said.

His face and light disappeared from the hole over Danny's head.

He kept staring upward at the blackness, trying to let the training he had from his Native American grandfather take over and control his breathing.

Right now, more than anything, he needed to just remain still and calm.

Standing on the narrow ledge fifty feet over rocks, holding on to roots for dear life, there was just nothing else he could do.

Then, he felt something again move across his foot in the pitch darkness of the jungle cavern.

It felt very real and had weight.

Then the horrible thing started up his leg.

24

September 17, 1970
Under the Lost City of Ishango, deep in the jungle of the Republic
of Congo

Danny pressed his back against the stone wall. He took a slow, shallow breath to try to stop himself from screaming and panicking. On a thin ledge, with only a bunch of roots holding him in place, he didn't dare panic. That would be the quickest way to get himself killed, no matter what was crawling up his leg.

Slowly, using his left hand to hold onto all the roots that had saved his life, he pressed his back against the rock wall then took a swipe at the creature as it came above his knee in the dark.

The back of his hand hit something fairly solid and covered in some sort of fur. It felt huge, but Danny figured it was about the size of his fist. More than likely one of the big spiders.

Whatever it was went flying off into the darkness. He just hoped it went far enough that it wasn't coming back.

He sure didn't need to be fighting a mad spider in the dark while clinging to the face of a cliff.

He took a deep breath and forced himself to try to calm his racing heart and try to listen.

Nothing seemed to be moving around him.

Only the distant sound of running water broke the intense silence.

Under the teeming masses, the river becomes clear, the path muddy.

That was the third Hydra Journals entry Danny's father had found in Cairo.

It was the riddle that had led them here, to this ancient lost city. The half million people who lived here when the Hydra Journals were written were the teeming masses. And now Danny could hear the river, or at least it sounded like a river.

He had no idea what "the path muddy" meant, but he had a hunch, as with anything in this adventure so far, it wasn't going to be easy to figure out.

And even here in the dark, pressed against a cliff face, he half expected the men from the Hydra League to show up. The League had seemed to be able to track them just about anywhere they went. Their only hope, Danny figured, was that the elephants had taken care of them. Otherwise, they would show up here soon, if they weren't already here somewhere, just watching them.

The Hydra League had been formed when this city was still alive and had a half million people in it. They clearly knew these ruins were here. They were the ones protecting the secret of the Fountain of Youth.

And they were the ones who had kidnapped Danny's father.

Danny figured the only way of ever seeing his father again was to stay alive long enough to find and solve all ten of the Hydra Journals' clues. A tall order for a guy stuck in the dark on a cliff ledge.

"Danny!" Craig shouted from above. "Hang on, we're coming!"

Danny glanced up as a number of torches lit up the hole above him.

"Careful on that floor," Danny shouted up to his friends. "More sections of it might give way."

"You found the way under the city I see," Hassett said as he poked his head over the edge and looked down.

"I think it found me," Danny said. "And I hear running water."

Hassett laughed. "Perfect. Hang on, we're hooking up enough rope to get you all the way to the ground."

"Not going anywhere," Danny said, trying to adjust his grip on the roots that he had been holding onto with a death grip for what seemed like an eternity now.

A moment later a rope started down toward Danny. Craig stuck his head over the edge and watched it.

"That's enough," Craig said as the rope with a few knots in it got to Danny's level. It looked to be a thick rope, clearly something Hassett had in his camp hidden in the center of the old city.

"How far down do you think it is from there?" Hassett called out.

"Fifty feet, maybe sixty!" Danny shouted back up, glancing down at his flickering torch on the rocks below.

"Hang on," Craig said.

Danny watched as he looked around, then leaned back over the edge. "Okay, we're ready. You want a ride down?"

"I would love one," Danny said.

Craig took the rope and got it swinging slightly until finally the end got close enough for Danny to reach with one hand.

"Are you ready?" Danny shouted back up. "It's going to have to hold all my weight."

Craig glanced back over his shoulder, then shouted down, "Ready."

"Here goes," Danny said.

Letting go of the roots, he grabbed the rope right above one of the knots tied in it and swung out into space, twisting in the hundreds of roots that filled the space. He wrapped his legs around the rope, like he had done in gym class in junior high.

He was living a childhood dream. He was in a jungle playing Tarzan, only he was underground, fifty feet above rocks, in the dark, with huge spiders, and scared to death.

Tarzan had it good.

The rope held and Danny swung through the maze of roots, breaking many of them, and wrapping others around his body. He used his arms to keep the roots away from his neck. The last thing he needed was to slip and have a root hang him.

He used his legs to support most of his weight on the rope, then with one hand he pulled off many of the roots before shouting, "Lower away!"

Less than five minutes later, he was on the rough rock surface of the cavern's floor.

He hadn't felt anything so good as solid ground under his feet. He hadn't realized until he was down just how frightened he had been. Now his hands started to shake.

"I'm down!" he shouted up to a tiny hole of light at least seven stories over his head.

All the way up, the rope had knots tied every five feet to make it easier to hold and climb. That was going to be a nasty climb to get back out of here.

"Tie the rope around a rock or anchor it in some way," Hassett shouted down, his voice echoing in the large, dark cavern.

Danny did as Hassett said, then shouted that it was secure.

"Coming down," Hassett shouted.

The old archeologist had a large pack on his back and he came down the rope like a monkey, faster than Danny could have done it. For a man in his sixties, Hassett was in great shape, that was for sure.

He got to the bottom and then worked on starting another few torches.

The twins followed next, dropping quickly hand-over-hand, clearly also used to climbing ropes. They both had packs of equipment as well. Bud came down next, with a bag of something in his mouth. He was slower, clearly more afraid of the height than of climbing down the rope. Craig was last and the slowest, not taking any chances.

Craig patted Danny on the shoulder after they were all standing on the rough floor of the cavern. "Glad you're all right."

"Thank all the roots," Danny said.

"Well, at least we found this," Hassett said, holding his torch up and studying the huge cavern around them. "The original residents clearly used these caverns."

He pointed to some old stone stairs leading down toward a lower cavern in the direction of the water, now clear in the light of six burning torches. The smoke from the torches twisted upward into the dark of the maze of roots.

Danny finally took time to really look around at the cavern he'd found.

Some of the walls were stone blocks as well. And part of the ceiling was the stone floor of the temple above them. A lot of rock had fallen in places, and the hole over their head seemed to be the only way out. The temple had been built over this cavern for a reason, of that there was no doubt. Now they just had to find the reason.

"Well," Craig said, shaking his head. "At least those Hydra League thugs won't find us down here."

"I wouldn't count on it," a distant voice said from over their heads.

All of their heads snapped to look up as if tied to the same string. There was a faint light in the hole above, and a few shadows moving around.

Danny knew that voice. It was the same man who had killed the professor back in Cairo.

How could they have found them?

Clearly they had escaped the elephants and had just been watching them the last few days.

As all six of them stared upward, the rope fell toward them, forming a huge pile with a thump at their feet.

The end had clearly been cut.

Now they had no way out.

"Enjoy your stay," the voice above them said.

Then he laughed, the sound echoing in the huge chamber like a bad villain in a bad movie.

Only this was real.

Very real.

25

September 17, 1970
Under the Lost City of Ishango, deep in the jungle of the Republic of Congo

"Have I said lately how screwed we are?" Craig said, staring at the pile of rope.

Above them the hole in the floor of the temple seemed like an impossible distance away to Danny. Totally impossible.

And the men that had been chasing them were up there, more than likely standing guard.

Before anyone else could say anything, Hassett held up his hand for all of them to remain silent. "We need to get away from this area quickly," he whispered. "Just in case they decide they need a little target practice."

Danny glanced back up. Hassett was right. Shooting them now would be like shooting fish in a bowl.

Hassett pointed to the rope on the ground. "Bring that." Then he motioned that they should follow him.

Danny picked up the huge pile of rope and his torch, and then he followed Hassett and the others down through the cavern, heading for old stone stairs that led deeper underground. At some point, the stairs must have led to something in the big cavern, but rocks now covered whatever it was.

Danny was glad that at least they were still alive. But they wouldn't be for long if they didn't find another way out of this cavern. Clearly, the two Hydra League men above didn't think there was another way out.

And Danny bet they knew the ruins.

The six of them quickly wound their way down through a series of linked smaller caverns, following the ancient stone path and stairs carved six thousand years before. Danny, on one trip to the Southwest, had gone into Carlsbad Caverns. These caverns seemed very much like those. The deeper they got underground, the more stalactites and stalagmites they wound their way through.

The colors of the stones shimmering in their torchlights were fantastic. Bright reds and blues and greens.

The deeper they got, the louder the sound of the river became, filling everything. If Danny hadn't been so worried about finding a way out, he would have enjoyed the cave exploring a lot more than he was.

Finally, the series of small caverns opened up into a huge cavern with a river running through one corner of it, crashing down over rocks and then disappearing into a wall, clearly going deeper in to the ground than it already was.

The stalactite-covered ceiling of the cavern was a good hundred feet over their heads. And from what Danny could see, there were a dozen smaller caverns leading off in different directions from this one. There was a maze of caverns under the ancient city. A maze that could easily get them lost forever.

Hassett, who had been leading them down the stone path of the ancient people, stopped in an open area and dropped the pack he had been carrying. "I don't think they can hear us down here."

"You think they're going to follow us?" Bud said.

Hassett shrugged. "Not for a week or so. Then they'll come looking for our bodies."

"Great," Craig said.

Danny glanced down at the river. "We have water, that's for sure. Anyone bring any food?"

"A day's worth for everyone," Hassett said.

Everyone else shook their heads no.

"We can stretch that to last a lot longer," Hassett said. "As long as we can drink that water."

"True," Bud said. "Many times I've gone without food for a week, but I had water."

Danny glanced at his short friend. He didn't want to know what the Cairo street kid had been through while trying to survive alone on the streets, but with comments like that, he was getting a good idea.

"So," Craig said, glancing at Danny, "what's the plan?"

Danny shrugged. "We find the next Hydra Journals entry. Then find a way out of here."

"How about we do both those things at the same time?" Bud asked.

"Seems like a good idea to me," Hassett said, smiling.

Danny agreed. They needed to find a new way out, since their way in was blocked to them, and more than likely guarded. Clearly, the ancient people used these caverns under their city, so it would be logical there would be more than one way in and out. If those ways were still open after six thousand years.

Ed glanced around, then quoted the third Hydra Journals entry. "Under the teeming masses, the river becomes clear, the path muddy."

"Shall we try to find the muddy path?" Ernie asked.

"As good a plan as any," Danny said. "And the farther we get from those men back there, the happier I will be."

"I'll second that," Craig said.

All six of them glanced back into the dark where they had come, then as one, they turned and headed down the stone pathway toward the loud river crashing over the rocks below them.

26

September 17, 1970
*Under the Lost City of Ishango, deep in the jungle of the Republic
of Congo*

"A path," Ed said an hour later.

Danny was up on some rocks above the river, climbing to see if he could see anything from a higher position that they had missed. The stone path they had followed down through the caverns had just ended at the edge of the river like a docking port.

But the river was tumbling over the rocks so hard just below the path that Danny couldn't imagine even taking a raft down that river and into the dark tunnel.

Hassett had suggested that back when the path was built, the river had been calmer, and the tunnel led to other caverns. Maybe, but Danny doubted it. Six thousand years just wasn't that long in the life of a river cutting through solid rock.

"It's a debarkation platform," Ernie had finally said after they had explored the edges of the tunnel below the platform. "The ancient people were coming from up the river to here."

There must be something back in the cavern they had started in that the ancient people would raft to here, then walk the rest of the way. Whatever it was had clearly been covered in cave-ins and rockslides. Danny hoped the next entry in the Hydra Journals wasn't back up there.

That was when they had focused their attention upstream and Ed had found the path.

Unlike the stone path they had come down into the cavern, this path was more natural and wound its way around and past rocks. The spray from the river caused it to be wet and slick and slightly muddy.

"Well," Craig said, "we found all the parts of the third Hydra Journals entry. Now what?"

"We follow the path," both Ernie and Ed said at the same time.

"Might as well," Danny said, glancing back up the cavern to where Bud had stationed himself as a lookout for the Hydra League goons. He waved for Bud to join them, then turned to everyone. "I want us all roped together in case we slip and fall in that river."

All of them agreed, and they waited until Bud joined them to put him in the middle.

"I'll lead," Danny said. "I'm a good swimmer. Dr. Hassett right behind me. Then Bud and the twins. Craig, you bring up the rear."

They all tied themselves into the heavy rope that they had lowered themselves into the cave with, spacing themselves four paces apart.

"Everyone be careful," Danny said. "Watch your step, but keep your eyes open for any ancient writing."

Danny took a couple of deep breaths, then, holding his torch high over his head to keep it as far from the river spray as he could, he started forward.

The path wound its way along the rocks just above the water. In the tunnel, the river seemed almost calm and very black. Danny had no desire to go in that cold water and find out what lived in there.

He wasn't thirty paces into the darkness of the river cave when he noticed two things. The first was a giant spider web across the path, its web glimmering in the faint light and dampness.

He eased forward and lit the bottom of the web on fire, using the flaring torch to break the web apart. Out of the corner of his eye he saw something move in the rocks, but he forced himself to not turn to look. It was just better to not know what lived down here in normally total blackness.

Then, as he held the torch out directly in front of him, he noticed it was blowing back slightly toward him, the smoke catching him in the eyes.

A breeze.

He stopped and glanced back along the trail where everyone else had stopped waiting for him to move forward. "Notice the breeze?"

"An opening somewhere ahead," Hassett said, smiling.

"Now if it is only big enough for us to get through," Ed said.

"We'll make it big enough," Ernie said.

Danny nodded, hoping Ernie was right.

Danny led the way along the slick, muddy path beside the river's edge. The path seemed to wind on forever. Clearly, this tunnel was not normally walked. There weren't any rapids in the river, so whoever used this usually floated down from some place up ahead.

"Any idea which direction we're heading?" Craig asked from behind Danny.

"I think we're going west," Dr. Hassett said. "Toward the mountains beside the city."

Danny didn't know if that was good or bad. He just kept going, moving slowly and carefully through the rocks.

Finally, just about at the point he was going to have them stop and rest, the tunnel opened up into a giant cavern.

Danny stepped a dozen steps out into the huge space, held up his torch, and stopped cold.

From what he could see, the cavern was huge, bigger than even a massive football stadium back home. On one edge, the river had turned into a decent-sized lake, with a high platform right in the center of the room beside the lake.

The platform faced a thousand stone seats that formed an amphitheatre around the platform.

"The Great Council Chamber," Dr. Hassett said beside Danny, his voice hushed. "We found the ancients' Great Council Chamber."

"There's got to be treasure here," Bud said.

"Amazing," Ernie said.

"A stunning find," Ed said.

"Wow! Big place," Craig said.

All Danny could do was stare.

And wish his father were here to see this.

27

September 17, 1970
Under the Lost City of Ishango, deep in the jungle of the Republic
of Congo

"What is the Great Council Chamber?" Danny asked Dr. Hassett after another minute of all of them staring at the huge cavern in front of them.

"From everything I can gather," Dr. Hassett said, "the ancient people who lived here and in other great cities around the globe were governed by a group of ten elders. These elders were elected and served like a city government, representing the adults, both men and women, of the city. This is where everyone met to listen to the council debate, act and vote."

Dr. Hassett pointed to the main platform beside the lake. "The Great Council would meet there and anyone who wanted could watch and listen. The important issues and elections would fill this place I'm sure. I had always hoped to find the remains of a Great Council Chamber, but never in this good a condition."

Dr. Hassett started off toward the huge platform beside the lake.

The floor of the cavern was paved in stone blocks and perfectly smooth. This entire room was an amazing piece of construction.

Danny and the rest followed, moving slowly, staring at everything around them.

Danny almost wanted to hold his breath as he climbed up the stone steps to the giant stage.

A stone table with a polished top filled the center of the stage, but nothing else was left but dust. After six thousand years of being in the open, even in a dark cave, that made sense. No wood or cloth would survive the moisture down here.

Behind the table on the stage was a stone wall. And across the top of the stone were carved hieroglyphs, large enough for everyone in the room to read, even from the top seats. It was the first writing of any type that Danny had seen in the ancient city.

Dr. Hassett, Ernie, and Ed stared at the hieroglyphs.

"What does it say?" Danny asked.

"Hopefully it's an exit sign with an arrow," Craig said.

"From the greatest city," Dr. Hassett said.

"No, highest city," Ed said, stopping him.

"I agree," Ernie said. "Not greatest, highest."

Dr. Hassett studied the carvings for a moment, then nodded. "From the highest city, power flows to the many."

"The fourth Hydra Journals entry?" Danny asked, sick to his stomach that it looked like the trail to rescue his father would end right here, in a cave deep under a jungle.

"More than likely, yes," Dr. Hassett said. "The ancient people wrote very little in stone. This is written in an early form of Egyptian hieroglyph, as the others were."

"Well, that's that," Craig said, sitting on the edge of the Great Council table. "That's not going to lead us anywhere."

Dr. Hassett looked at Craig, then at Danny and laughed. "Of course it is."

"From the highest city, power flows to the many," Danny said, repeating the phrase. "Assuming we can get out of this cave, how is that going to help us?"

Again Dr. Hassett laughed and even Ernie and Ed looked puzzled. "Danny, your father and I both believed that this ancient civilization existed, and we both believed that it spanned the globe and was of a high degree of engineering and civilization before it died off for some reason. Many different races are descendants of this first civilization, and many races built in their ruins."

Danny nodded, as did Ernie and Ed.

"That was in my father's notebooks," Danny said.

Dr. Hassett pointed back at the images carved in the stone over the great stage. "The highest city?"

Suddenly Danny realized what Dr. Hassett was talking about. "Machu Picchu?"

"Exactly," Dr. Hassett said.

"But wasn't that an Inca city?" Craig asked.

"Later," Dr. Hassett said. "The Incas took it over, built new parts, and made it their own. But there is much evidence that the city was older than the early Incas."

"Power flows to the many?" Danny asked.

Dr. Hassett shrugged. "That's something you'll have to figure out there."

"So the next clue is in the Andes?" Bud asked.

Danny nodded. "Looks that way."

"Great," Bud said. "Glad we found it and figured it out. But right now we're trapped a long way underground in the center of Africa with bad men stalking us. First things first, I always say."

None of them had an argument for that.

28

September 17, 1970
Under the Lost City of Ishango, deep in the jungle of the Republic
of Congo

As Dr. Hassett, Ernie, and Ed studied the rest of the main platform of the ancient council chamber for any other clues to anything, Danny decided that he and Bud and Craig would look for the way out.

Danny watched as Craig held his torch up. The faint smoke from it drifted to his right and toward the tunnel they had come through.

The three of them climbed down off the large stone platform. "Craig," Danny said, "go toward the left wall. Bud, you go up the right staircase, I'll go up the left. Using the smoke from our torches, we should be able to get some sort of reading on where the draft is coming from."

Danny quickly climbed the stone staircase that went upward between the stone benches. Even fifty rows up in the stands, he could clearly hear everything Dr. Hassett and the twins were saying. Amazing acoustics in this cave, that was for sure.

He stood about halfway up the staircase and let the air around him calm, watching the smoke. It drifted still toward the tunnel, so the entrance was above him.

"Nothing down here," Craig said from down by the left wall. "Smoke just sort of swirls."

"Mine shows the entrance is up top," Bud said.

"Go slow," Danny said, turning and starting up. "We may have someone waiting for us up there."

Bud nodded and moved at the same pace as Danny up the staircase.

At the top, there was a wide area inside yet another cavern. The entire floor of this cavern had also been paved with stones. The breeze felt clearly more noticeable, and the air was warmer as well.

Craig joined Bud and Danny in the center of the room. They let the air settle, then headed to where the wind was coming from.

At the back of the room were over a dozen tunnels, some made of stone blocks, others cut out of the natural stone. All of them led off the back of the room like spokes on a wheel. Clearly, at one point there had been a lot of entrances to this great chamber, so that a lot of people could come in at once. But now the breeze was only coming from one.

Bud led the way, moving so silently that after a moment, he motioned for Danny and Craig to just stop and he would scout it out. Danny watched Bud's torch disappear around a corner in the stone tunnel.

The waiting seemed to stretch as Danny worked to not hold his breath as he tried to listen for any problems Bud might have.

Then, after what must have been the longest two or three minutes on record, Bud came back, smiling.

"The tunnel was blocked at the entrance a long time ago," Bud said. "Clearly on purpose, so no one would find this place."

"That doesn't sound good," Craig said.

"There was a cave-in just short of the blocked entrance," Bud said, smiling. "We can climb up the rocks and get out just fine."

"Okay, so we can get out," Craig said, clearly feeling as relieved as Danny felt. "Now what do we do next?"

"We look for treasure," Bud said, smiling.

"Besides that," Craig said, laughing.

"I think that's a discussion for everyone," Danny said. "But I'm voting for South America."

"Yeah," Craig said. "Why did I know that?"

Two hours later, sitting on the benches of an ancient civilization's Great Council Chamber, they worked out their plan.

29

September 22, 1970
Bunia, Republic of the Congo, on the shores of Lake Albert

Four days after leaving the Great Council Chamber, they made it back down the Trail of Elephants to the shores of Lake Albert.

Dr. Hassett left them almost at once, headed back down the Nile. He didn't dare stay since he was easily recognized in the area. He planned on holing up in an apartment in London and writing up his notes and publishing a few papers on the great lost city. He had enough pictures, enough evidence, that he hoped to get some decent publications, even though his name had been discredited.

Danny wasn't happy with him leaving them, but they really didn't have any choice if they didn't want to draw attention to themselves. With luck, they would meet him in London after they had found the next Hydra Journals' entry in Machu Picchu.

The problem they faced was how to get out of Africa.

At first it had been suggested by Bud that they try to make it across the Congo and to the west coast, but that was ruled out by everyone.

Even Danny knew enough about that jungle and the tribes and governments of the Congo to not go that way.

And none of the boys wanted to try going back down the Nile to Cairo, following Dr. Hassett. Going that way felt to Danny like walking into a huge trap.

Right now, he was convinced that if they stayed hidden, they would have a head start on the Hydra League men still guarding their old camp up in the ruins. It would still be days, maybe weeks yet, before those men discovered that they hadn't died in the cave, but had escaped.

After leaving the cave, Bud had worked his way back down into their old camp in the ruins. The two Hydra League men had been sleeping close by, so Bud had managed to get all their money and a few personal things in packs that the two men wouldn't know were missing. So at least they had money for whatever they needed to do.

"We go east," Ed said after they had all stared at the maps for a time.

"Aren't we trying to go west?" Craig asked. "Seems that South America is west of here, if I remember my world map correctly."

Danny agreed. "Going east across the Indian Ocean and then the Pacific is a long way out of the way."

Ed nodded. "But we need to go east to get out of Africa. Then we go south and west."

"I agree," Ernie said. He pointed at the huge body of water on the map. "We need to cross Lake Victoria and get into Kenya."

Ed traced the path they were proposing with his finger on the map. "We land in Kisumu in Kenya, take overland transportation of some sort to Nairobi, then a train down to Mombasa on the coast. From there we can get a ship to take us down the coast to South Africa. In Cape Town, we know people who will help us get to Brazil."

Danny looked at the two twins shocked that they would even think of the idea. "You can't go back to South Africa."

"Yeah," Bud said. "They were shooting at you in Cairo, remember?"

Both Ed and Ernie nodded. "We don't have a choice. It is our best chance from here."

Danny didn't like it, but after a few hours of studying the maps, he knew they were right. The twins had to go right back into what might be a death trap if they were all to get out of Central Africa and get on with the search for the Hydra Journals.

30

October 2, 1970
Cape Town, South Africa

The freighter docked at just after twelve noon in what was clearly a huge, industrial port to one side of Cape Town. From the deck of the freighter as they moved into the harbor, Danny could see at least a hundred ships of all sizes, if not more. It was a very busy international port.

The city itself looked beautiful, tucked in under a long mountain with a flat top the twins said was aptly named Table Mountain. Ernie pointed out Devil's Peak and Signal Hill to the right of Table Mountain. The place would have been interesting to explore if it wasn't so deadly to the twins. They had to get in and out of this port fast.

The sun was high overhead and the air was hot and thick with the smell of oil and sewage. Hundreds of workers swarmed over the docks, loading and unloading the ships.

Danny and Craig were standing on the deck as the crew finished the tying up of the ship. Ed and Ernie had insisted that as a group, they couldn't be seen together. Only Danny and Craig dared do anything, so the twins, with Bud, had stayed hidden below decks, with Bud standing guard for them.

With the apartheid form of government, and the high levels of segregation, two white boys and two black boys were not allowed together. Just doing that would be enough to get Ed and Ernie tossed in jail, and then once the police discovered who they were, they would be killed without trial.

So it was up to Danny and Craig to find a British ship of some kind and book them all passage to Brazil. Danny had no doubt, looking at the busy docks, that wasn't going to be an easy task.

An hour later, they finally found the headquarters of a British ship company, tucked just off the docks on a side street.

The man inside, behind the desk, was dressed in a blue uniform of some sort, with a tie and hat. A fan was working hard in the window to keep the air in the room moving, but it still felt like a sauna bath in the small office.

Danny introduced himself and Craig and told the man that they and three other friends were looking for a way to get to Brazil.

"Americans?" the man said in a fairly proper British accent.

Danny nodded. "Washington State."

The man nodded and chuckled to himself. "We get a lot of American boys these days, traveling the world, trying to stay out of your infernal war in Southeast Asia. Do you have money or do you need to work your way there?"

"We have some money," Danny said. "But we don't need anything fancy. In fact, we would rather not be on a fancy ship."

"Hiding are we?" the man asked, looking at them.

"In a manner of speaking," Danny said, letting the man go ahead and think they were running away from the draft. It was easier than telling him the truth.

The man nodded. "I have a freighter leaving in two days for Brazil. It will be running mostly empty to pick up coffee. I have two spare crew cabins you could have."

"That would be perfect," Danny said.

"All five of you need to be on dock 86-B before seven in the morning, October 4th, with your passports."

"Not a problem," Danny said.

"See to it that it isn't," the man said.

The five tickets cost Danny almost half of the money he had left, but it was worth it. And once in Brazil or Peru, he could wire Uncle Steve and get more.

"That went surprisingly easy," Craig said as he and Danny headed back toward the freighter.

"Yeah, now we just have to hide for the next two days. And try to keep the twins from being spotted."

"From the sounds of it," Craig said, shaking his head, "just being seen with us could be just as bad."

"Yeah," Danny said.

In America, he had watched night after night of civil rights demonstrations on television. He had watched the replay of the assassination of Martin Luther King. Being part Indian, he understood some of what the blacks were going through, but not much. He had been lucky to be raised where he had been raised.

And until Ed and Ernie had mentioned that they couldn't be seen together, Danny hadn't even thought of them as anything but two others his age. Sometimes the world was just a stupid place.

As Danny and Craig moved between two large crates and were just about to step into the open in front of the freighter, Bud appeared beside them.

"Stop! Hide!"

He motioned for them to duck back in behind the crates.

Just as they did, two white men in brown dock police uniforms escorted Ed and Ernie past the crates.

Both men were carrying guns, and had them pointed at the twins.

Danny could feel his stomach twist. They couldn't lose the twins now. They had to do something.

"What happened?" Danny whispered.

"Captain turned them in as being suspicious," Bud whispered back, spitting on the ground in disgust. "I barely got away."

"As soon as they find out who they really are, they're dead," Craig said.

"I know," Danny said, doing his best to keep his heart from beating right out of his chest. He was sweating harder than he should be in the heat. "We follow them."

Bud nodded and led out, motioning to them when it was clear or not.

They didn't have far to follow the two policemen. The twins were taken into a large warehouse two ships down from where their freighter had docked. On the small side door of the warehouse, a sign said simply, "Port Police."

Danny had no doubt that the twins were as good as dead unless he and Craig and Bud could do something, and do it fast.

But what? Danny had no idea.

31

October 2, 1970
Cape Town, South Africa

The policeman raised his gun at Danny Hawk and shouted, "Halt!"

Danny stopped, then carefully turned and raised his hands above his head.

Never, in all his life, had he been so scared. He had been in a lot of rough situations over the years, and even more since his father had gone missing. But having some large man in a brown uniform point a gun at him was the most frightening.

Around him, the huge three-story tall warehouses of the Cape Town shipping docks felt like huge child's blocks. They blocked the sun from getting down into the narrow alleys between the buildings, but didn't block the heat. And right now, Danny had sweat running down the side of his face. He wasn't sure if it was from the heat, or from the fear.

Probably both.

If this plan didn't work, he just might spend a lot of years in a South African prison. And right now, standing here with his hands in the air and a gun pointed at him, he wasn't sure about anything work-ing, let alone getting his friends, Ed and Ernie Black out of jail.

For all Danny knew, he might be shot where he stood.

"What are you doing down here?" the man asked, not lowering his gun. The guy was huge, carried the gun like it was a toy, and looked mean, with a pockmarked face and balding head.

"Looking for my dad, sir," Danny said, in his best British accent, following the cover story he and Craig and Bud had decided on earlier. "He was supposed to be down here. His name is Carl Conley. My name's Carl Conley Junior."

Carl Conley was a name Bud had seen on an office sign near the dock headquarters. The guy either ran this entire docking facility, or was near the top. Danny had no idea if he had a son or not, but he had to take a chance that the guard wouldn't know if the big boss did or not. After all, this was a huge docking facility.

The guard lowered his gun instantly and smiled a sickly smile. "Oh, sorry. I was just doing my job, you understand."

Danny took a deep breath and lowered his hands, going on with the plan he, Bud, and Craig had come up with. "No harm done."

Bud had said that the best plan was the boldest plan. Right now, Danny didn't feel so bold. He just hoped the guard didn't notice that his hands were shaking.

The guard put his gun away and then smiled again, stepping closer to Danny. "Any idea where your father was supposed to be?"

"His secretary said he was going to be at a jail," Danny said, continuing his bold lie. "I think she called it a holding area. She said it was in one of the warehouse buildings. He was coming down to see two prisoners. She gave me directions to the building, but I got lost."

Danny knew he was only one building over from the jail holding the twins.

"You didn't miss it by much, young man," the guard said, laughing. "And don't worry on getting lost. I still get turned around in this maze of buildings and I've worked here for years. Follow me."

He led the way between the two buildings and then to a door in the side of one warehouse that Danny had seen the twins taken through.

Danny walked in ahead of the guard, trying to act like he belonged where he was.

The small jail was just like an office, with two desks, a few extra guns on the wall, and a refrigerator tucked down a small hall behind one desk. The small window was barred and dirty.

The place was stuffy, hot, and smelled stale and sickly, like some drunk had thrown up the night before.

Another large guard sat behind the desk to the right, and through a barred window in a door behind him, Danny could see one of the twins in a windowless cell.

"Conley is on his way down here," the guard who had escorted Danny into the room said to his friend. "This is his kid."

The guard behind the desk stared at Danny, clearly not believing his story.

Danny knew he looked rough and his clothes were slightly dirty from being in the jungle, even though they had managed to wash most of their things while on the ship from Kenya. Danny knew he didn't look like an executive's son.

"Thought Conley's kid was younger," the guard behind the desk said, frowning and looking at Danny carefully.

This was going badly. This guy knew Conley.

"I grew up," Danny said, shrugging.

Suddenly, a loud crash filled the room. Something large had slammed against the building near the jail door.

Danny ducked for cover behind the desk, still playing his part, acting like he was suddenly afraid. Both guards headed for the door, guns drawn. Danny just hoped Craig and Bud stayed out of sight.

As the two guards reached the door, another crash echoed from the next building.

"Stay here, kid," one guard said to Danny over his shoulder as they went outside on the run.

The moment they went through the door, leaving it wide open,

Danny headed for the twins. The keys to the jail cell were hanging on a peg beside the door and Danny grabbed them.

Outside, one of the guards swore in pain.

Clearly, Craig and Bud were distracting them. Danny wasn't sure he wanted to know how. Bud had said to trust him, the guards would be distracted.

Danny sprinted into the darker cell area.

Ed was in the cell to the right, Ernie to the left. The place smelled of urine and vomit.

"Danny!" Ed said, moving to the bars.

"What are you doing here?" Ernie said.

Both looked shocked and very happy.

"Jailbreak," Danny said. "But if we don't move fast, I'm going to join you."

And Danny didn't like the sound of that at all.

32

October 2, 1970
Cape Town, South Africa

There was another crash outside as Danny fumbled with the keys. He finally found the right one after what seemed like an eternity and opened Ed's cell door.

From outside, one of the guards again swore in pain. Then there was a gunshot.

The sound froze all three of them.

Danny's stomach twisted even tighter at the thought of Bud or Craig getting shot.

"Hurry," Ernie said as Danny again fumbled with the keys.

"I'll get our passports and papers," Ed said, sprinting for the front office. "I saw where the guard put them."

More swearing and shouting from outside, this time a little more distant.

Danny finally got Ernie's door open and the two of them ran for the outer office.

Ed slammed a drawer and held up his and Ernie's papers with a smile. "Got them, and the money those two took from us as well."

At the outer door, Danny had the twins stop and he went out first, looking around. No sign of either of the guards. Just sounds of swearing from the other side of the warehouse across the paved alleyway.

There was no one else in sight.

The plan had been for Craig and Bud to lead the two men to the west, while Danny and the twins went in the opposite direction. They were to meet up somewhere near dock 86-B.

Danny indicated that the twins should follow him, then at a run, they turned left and went down the side of the warehouse, then a quick left again around a corner of the building. They ran for the length of two large warehouses, turned right, ran the length of yet another, and then turned left again.

Danny was really starting to get winded in the heat when Ed said, "In here."

They ducked into an area between two buildings that was stacked with dozens of piles of wooden pallets.

"You are amazing!" Ed said breathlessly to Danny, patting him on the back.

"We thought we were dead for sure," Ernie said.

"We all might be if we don't find a good hiding place," Danny said, looking both ways down the narrow alley between the warehouses. He was sweating so hard, it was stinging his eyes. They all were going to need something to drink pretty soon as well in this heat.

"We can't keep going together," Ed said.

Ernie nodded. "This is still South Africa. Whites and blacks can't be together doing anything, unless the white is in charge."

Danny just shook his head. He understood the reality of that, but he sure hated it. Just as he hated it when people treated him differently, or put him down for his Native American heritage.

"Where are we meeting Bud and Craig?" Ernie asked.

"And how are we getting out of here?"

Danny explained that he had booked them all passage on a British freighter heading for South America, but it didn't leave port until 7 A.M. October 4th.

"That's two nights and a day away," Ernie said.

Danny nodded. He knew that, and was very worried about that as well. This was a very busy port, well-patrolled. Now that the twins had escaped, everyone would be looking for all of them. Hiding was going to be a real problem. Just getting to dock 86-B was going to be a problem. That was a good mile from where they were.

"Here," Ed said, pointing back at the pile of wooden pallets.

Danny, at first, couldn't figure out what Ed meant. This alley clearly wasn't a good hiding place. And it was far too close to those two guards back there.

Then Ed moved to a dolly with four wheels and a handle. There were three of them parked in the alley.

"Pallet movers," Ernie said to his twin brother. "Great thinking."

"Want to clue me in?" Danny asked.

"Watch," Ed said. He grabbed one machine, quickly moved it around like he had handled the thing before. It had two long blades on the front that slipped in under the bottom pallet. With a few quick pumps on a handle, Ed picked up a six foot high stack of empty pallets.

Ernie quickly did the same thing, rolling the pallets out into the open.

"Now, you walk behind us, pretending like you're in charge of what we're doing," Ed said. "We're taking these to dock 86-B."

"You're the boss," Ernie said firmly to Danny, looking him right in the eye. "Remember that and act that way."

"I hate this," Danny said.

Ed smiled. "This is what our parents fought against and died trying to stop."

"Some day it will stop," Ernie said. "But for now, we live with it and get out of this country."

"Can't be fast enough for me," Danny said.

33

October 2, 1970
Cape Town, South Africa

The three of them got a few odd looks from other workers along the way, but no one stopped them. Danny hated acting like he was in charge of his two friends just because of their skin color. But he tried to, and Ernie and Ed pulled the stacks of pallets carefully, slumping over like they were used to the hard work.

Finally, as they neared the dock where the British freighter would hopefully take them out of this country, Danny heard Bud whisper from a nearby open warehouse door.

"Here."

Danny and the twins glanced over to where Bud was in the dark shadows just inside a warehouse door.

The twins quickly moved the wooden pallets over into an area that held other pallets, then the three of them went inside.

It took a minute for Danny's eyes to adjust. But it soon became clear that the warehouse was stacked completely full of huge crates.

Some of the stacks reached clear to the tall ceiling three stories overhead.

The air inside was cooler than outside, but not by much.

The huge shipping doors of the warehouse were closed, and the only light came from a few high, dirty windows.

"Is Craig all right?" Danny asked as Bud led them deeper into the darkness of the warehouse.

"We heard shots," Ernie said.

"Just fine," Craig said, stepping out of the shadows. "Can't say that I like getting shot at by the police, though."

Danny patted his best friend on the shoulder. "Just think of all the stories we can tell the girls when we get home."

Craig laughed. "Yeah, like they're going to believe us."

Danny laughed as well, very happy to see his best friend alive and well.

"I've found a great place to hide," Bud said.

He led them, single-file, deeper into the giant stacks of crates until they were near the middle-back of the warehouse. Then Bud pointed upward.

"We climb up there and hide on top, or inside those top crates, depending on what's in them. We'll know if workers start moving these things. We'll have time to make a break for it. And guards aren't going to climb every stack in here looking for us."

"Perfect," Ed said, nodding.

"But we're going to need water," Ernie said.

Danny looked up at the tall stacks of wooden crates towering over them. He wasn't real excited about spending the next two nights in here, but at this point, they had no choice.

Or at least none that he could think of.

"The next warehouse over has an office in it," Bud said, pointing to the west wall. "I'm sure we can find water there at night, after everyone's gone. And we have enough food to last us until we get on board the ship."

With that, Bud turned and started up the side of the stack of huge wooden crates like he was climbing the side of a rock mountain. It was as if Bud had spent most of his life climbing wooden crates. He didn't miss a step or a handhold and before Danny realized it, Bud went over the top and disappeared.

A moment later he poked his head back over the edge. "Easy. Everyone take their own stack. But these things are so close together, if we have to, we can run across the top of them."

Danny remembered the terror he had felt jumping from one roof to another over an alley in Cairo. He really didn't like the idea of jumping from crate to crate over a thirty-foot drop.

But so far, in looking for his father, he'd done a lot of things he didn't think he'd ever do. He just hoped crate-jumping ahead of guards with guns wouldn't turn out to be one of them.

34

October 3, 1970
Cape Town, South Africa

The first night sleeping on the tops of the tall stacks of crates had been nerve-wracking. The crates were square, and Danny could barely lie side to side without his head or feet being near an edge. So all night he had a constant fear of falling asleep and rolling off.

He had managed to use a few of his clothes from his bag as padding and a pillow, but the rough surface of the wooden crate top still dug into his skin every time he moved. And any noise from outside the huge warehouse made them all sit up and hold their breaths in the dark. The dock was a busy place, day and night, so there were a lot of noises.

It had been a very long night.

After what seemed like an eternity, the sun finally came up, casting bright streams of light through the huge warehouse. From on top of the crates, the place looked more like a giant checkerboard, with the spaces between the crates dark lines. Since the tall stacks weren't much more than four feet apart, all of them had gotten used to jumping over the dark between the crates. It had twisted Danny's stomach the first few times, but now he knew it was nothing more than a really wide step to get from one to another.

Bud had vanished without a word just as the first light of day was starting to color the dirty windows of the warehouse. Now, suddenly, he appeared from out of the dark near Danny's crate.

"The British ship docked last night," Bud said. "They're just finishing unloading it now."

Danny had been worried a lot about how they were going to board tomorrow morning, in the light, with all the dock hands around getting ready for the ship's departure.

"I think," Danny said, "that when it calms down some around the ship, I should go talk with the captain. See if we can board late tonight."

"Good idea," Ernie said. "Better than in the light."

"We can go on separately as well," Ed said. "Less chance of us being noticed that way."

"And I'm going with you to talk to the captain," Craig said. "Less chance of a policeman paying attention if there are two of us."

"I'll make sure there are no police around before you go," Bud said.

"Good," Craig said. "I can't say I was looking forward to another night on top of this wooden mountain."

Everyone agreed to that, then talked softly for a while about what might be the best time to board if the captain of the ship allowed it. They decided that around eleven would be the best, since that appeared to be when there was a shift change of workers and thus the fewest number of people around.

For the rest of the morning, they all tried to sleep some more. Then, just after one in the afternoon, with the twins staying up on their crates, Bud gave the all clear.

Danny and Craig climbed down and strode out into the heat, headed for the ship, pretending to act like they belonged there and knew what they were doing.

There were a few dock workers a good warehouse distance away, but no one seemed to be anywhere near the British ship.

Danny felt really exposed out on the dock beside the huge ship, and even more obvious walking across the long plank way up to the ship's deck.

"Are we supposed to ask for permission to board?" Craig asked as they neared the edge of the ship.

Danny shrugged. "I have no idea, but I would think so."

"I don't see a doorbell," Craig said.

"Or even a place to knock," Danny said, looking both directions along the ship as they hesitated before stepping on board. He had a hunch they would be doing something wrong if they went on board without someone's permission, so he decided they would just stop and wait.

They stood there for a good thirty seconds, both of them looking around, not only for someone on the ship, but for guards with guns to come running in their direction along the dock.

No one seemed to notice them.

"Now I know what a target on a shooting range feels like," Craig said.

"Let's give it another minute, then board and find someone," Danny said. He was sweating in the hot sun and for the second time in two days, his hands were shaking.

At that moment, a voice with a clear British accent echoed down at them from up near the top of what looked like the bridge of the ship. "Permission to come aboard. Come to the top level."

Danny didn't see who shouted, but waved his hand in acknowledgement, then he and Craig boarded the big freighter.

The ship was long, with open holds in the front and back decks, and a three-story center area. Their footsteps echoed on the metal decking and it seemed even hotter on the ship than it had been on the dock, if that was possible.

"You ever get the feeling we're going from the frying pan into the fire?" Craig asked.

"In more ways than one," Danny said. "More ways than one."

35

October 3, 1970
Cape Town, South Africa

Inside the steel-plated structure, it wasn't any cooler. In fact, it seemed to be warmer.

"I hope our cabins have air-conditioning," Craig said softly as they climbed the metal staircase.

"Dreaming again," Danny said.

Craig made a snorting sound. "I used to dream of girls and football."

There was nothing Danny could say to that. Because his best friend had come with him, Craig had been shot at more than once, been trapped in a cave, had to jump off a moving ferry, and run from gunmen from the top of one building roof to another. Danny couldn't ask for a better friend, of that he had no doubt.

The upper deck had doors and windows open, and a slight breeze was blowing through the bridge area, cooling it a little.

"Come on in," a man in a blue uniform said from what looked to be the bridge area. The windows were huge along the front, and there was a giant wheel with a chair behind it square in the middle. The panels under the windows were filled with instruments the entire width of the room. And there was another big table along the back wall that held maps and charts. Hundreds of them from what Danny could tell.

"I'm Captain Townsend," the man said in a clear British accent. He smiled and extended his hand. "I assume you are two of my passengers to South America."

Danny and Craig both shook his hand as Danny did the introductions. The captain's hand was firm and calloused. He was shorter than Danny by a few inches and looked stout, as if he hadn't missed a meal in a long time. His uniform jacket was tight, and his tie slightly loose. Danny couldn't even imagine wearing a jacket and tie in this heat, but the captain didn't even seem to be sweating.

"Ya know," Captain Townsend said, smiling, showing a mouthful of really brown and twisted teeth, "I admire a man who has respect for another man's ship. So, what can I do for you boys? You know we don't set sail until tomorrow morning?"

"Yes, sir, we do," Danny said. "But we were hoping we could board later tonight, to stay out of the way tomorrow morning. We'd stay in our cabins and be no problem, I can assure you."

The captain looked first at Danny, then at Craig, no longer smiling. "The ticket master said you American boys were on the run from something. Now that wouldn't be serving your country, would it?"

Danny shook his head. "No, sir. We are both in college and not needed for military service."

Now the captain really frowned. Danny had a hunch he had clearly been ready to give them a long lecture on duty to a country.

"I don't much like taking on trouble on my ship. If not service, then what are you running from?"

Danny glanced at Craig, who just shrugged. Danny had no intention of going through the long story of the Hydra League, but he could tell the captain a little of the truth. Selected parts.

"I'm looking for my father," Danny said. "He disappeared in Cairo a number of months ago. We have information that leads us to believe he was taken to Peru. Four of my friends are helping me on this search."

The captain nodded and just waited for Danny to go on. This man was clearly very smart.

"Craig and I are from Washington State, and while in Cairo, we met Bud and the twins, Ed and Ernie. Bud is from Cairo and Ed and Ernie are from here. They are all about our age."

Now the captain was nodding, as if he was ahead of Danny's story, but still waiting.

"Ed and Ernie are black," Danny said, watching the captain's face. The man didn't seem to have a reaction, so Danny went on. "Their parents were killed by the South African government for protesting against apartheid. The government here is looking for them as well."

"For heaven's sake, son, why did you boys come back here then?"

"We were in Kenya," Danny said, changing the truth of his story a little to make it easier to tell. No point in telling him about a hidden city in the jungles of the Congo. "That was where we discovered we needed to go to Peru in my father's search."

Again, the captain nodded. "And you had to change ships here? Now I see why you want to come on board tonight."

"Sleeping on a wooden crate in a warehouse can get tiring," Craig said, smiling.

The captain laughed. "I can see why it would. But you are putting yourselves and your friends at great risk by telling me this."

He moved over a few feet and picked up a piece of paper. On it in big red letters was the word 'Wanted.'

The captain gave the paper to Danny. "It says there your two friends escaped from a dock jail yesterday, with the help of at least two white boys."

Now the captain was no longer smiling.

Danny felt his stomach clamp up into a knot. He forced himself to try to breathe, but he didn't get much of the warm air.

"Have I said lately how screwed we are?" Craig muttered, staring at the wanted poster.

Danny ignored his friend and squarely faced the captain, looking him in the eye. "Yes, sir, the twins were taken by port security because of their skin color and the fact that our last captain said they looked suspicious. If the government had discovered who they were, they would have been killed without trial. I was the one who broke them out of that cell."

"We all helped," Craig said, smiling a sickly smile.

"As I said, I don't like trouble on my ship," the captain said. He stared at Danny for a minute. Then he nodded. "But I like the policies of this South African government even less. Half my crew is colored, or as they are wanting to be called now, black. My first mate has a dark skin color because he has a father from Pakistan. I hate even docking here."

He took the paper back from Craig and wadded it up into a ball and tossed it into a nearby garbage can. "Come on board tonight at eleven during dock shift changes," the captain said, his voice very serious. "Your cabins are numbered seven and eight on the deck below this one. Stay inside until we are at sea and someone comes for you."

"Thank you, sir," Danny said.

The captain nodded. "Just don't make me sorry I'm doing this."

36

October 3, 1970
Cape Town, South Africa

That night at eleven, Danny went on board first and alone, greeted by the captain. "I got most of my crew below securing the cargo. Make it quick."

Danny nodded and waved for the rest to come forward. The captain sounded as worried as Danny felt. That wasn't a good sign.

Craig came from the right and was halfway up the gang plank when Ernie appeared out of the shadows and came up the plank behind Craig. Both of them had disappeared with a quick thank you to the captain when Ed appeared and came on board, followed quickly by Bud. It all took less than a minute.

"Stay hidden until we come to get you," the captain said to Danny as he turned away to let Danny follow Bud inside.

The cabins were warm, but not unbearable. Ed and Ernie took one with only two bunks, Craig, Bud, and Danny took the other one that had three.

As Danny closed the door, Bud dropped onto the bunk. "I hope prison beds are this comfortable."

"I don't like this," Bud said, walking around in a circle in the middle of the room like a caged animal would walk. "We are trapped here, trusting the honor of a British captain."

"If we're going to get out of this country," Danny said, "we don't have a choice."

None of them slept during the next six hours. Danny just sat on a bunk facing the door, expecting it to be opened at any moment by a South African policeman with a big gun.

Bud alternated between pacing and sitting on the floor in the corner. Craig just lay on his bunk staring at the ceiling. They didn't talk. They felt like they didn't dare.

It was still two hours from sailing when the door did burst open, but it wasn't the South African police, but the captain. "Quickly, bring your things. You have to hide."

Danny scrambled to his feet, grabbing the case with the copies of his father's notebooks and his clothes bag, then went out the door behind the captain, a half step ahead of Bud.

The captain said the same thing to the twins, then without waiting to see if he was being followed, went down the hallway to a staircase and then started down.

He didn't stop at the main deck, but kept going down the tight, circular metal staircase.

Danny lost track of how far they went down, but clearly they were going down into the cargo hold.

At the bottom, the captain shoved open a hatch and went through, waiting until all five boys had followed him.

The inside of the freighter's cargo hold was almost as large as the warehouse, and just about as tall. Lights were strung along the ceiling and they gave the place a dim, eerie glow.

Parts of the cargo hold were stacked with the same kind of crates they had spent the night before on. They were all well tied down to the walls and each other. It seemed the big wooden things were standard shipping crates for this area of the world.

The captain pointed to the large stacks of crates secured against a bulkhead. "Climb up on top and stay very silent and out of sight, no matter what you hear. We're done loading this area, but there will be inspectors walking through."

With that, he ducked back through the hatch toward the stairs and slammed the hatch closed.

Thirty seconds later, they were all on top of different crates and had their gear stored on the bulkhead side.

Up that high in the cargo hold, the temperature was higher than it had been outside on the deck. Danny didn't much like the idea of them being trapped down here, but again, he could see no choice.

On the crate beside Danny, Craig stretched out staring at the deck over him, his head resting on a folded up shirt.

"How much did you say you paid for these tickets?"

All Danny could think to say was *Hopefully not with our lives.* So instead, he said nothing.

37

October 4, 1970
Cape Town, South Africa

One very long hour later, the hatch below clanged open.

Danny didn't dare glance over the edge, but from the sounds of it, there were three men down there.

They walked around and down the narrow aisle through the middle of the hold between the cargo, then came back.

"Satisfied now, Commander?"

It was the captain's voice.

"They have not yet boarded, and we depart in an hour. As I have said, the ticket agent told them seven, so my guess is that is when you will see them, if they are stupid enough to try to still board after what I understand happened yesterday."

"Thank you, Captain," another man said, his voice low and cold. "We will wait for them on deck. I assume you are correct. These five boys are proving to be very resourceful."

"Yes, very," another man's voice said.

Danny almost choked.

The voice was the same one Danny had heard in Cairo ordering the professor's death. And the same one he had heard before the rope into the cavern was cut.

Somehow, the Hydra League had followed them here.

How was that possible?

And how could the Hydra League be working with South African police?

The sound of movement came from below, then finally the hatch was slammed closed again.

Bud eased silently toward the edge of the crate he was on top of and peeked down.

Danny held his breath and waited.

He was in a cargo hold of a ship in Cape Town, South Africa, and the Hydra League had almost found him. There was going to be nowhere on the planet they could run from these men.

"Clear," Bud whispered.

"Was that who I think it was?" Craig whispered.

Danny nodded, trying to force himself to breathe and calm down.

"Hydra League?" Ernie asked.

"How?" Ed asked.

"At least when we don't get on board, they will stay in South Africa looking for us," Bud said.

"Don't count on it," Danny said.

Craig let out a long breath. "Have I said lately just how screwed we are?"

38

October 4, 1970
Middle of the South Atlantic

Seven hours later, no one had come for them.

An hour after their visitors, the ship had clearly left the dock.

For the first few hours, it felt as if the ship was moving slowly through the huge harbor. Then, in the fourth hour, the ship clearly got to rougher open seas.

It got almost impossible to stay on top of the crates with the ship rolling from side to side, so they all climbed down and found hidden areas on the deck surface among the cargo.

"How long does it take to reach international waters?" Craig finally asked after seven hours in the cargo hold.

"We should be well into them by now," Ed said from where he and his brother were hiding between two crates.

"I agree," Ernie said.

"So how come the captain hasn't come for us?" Bud asked.

"I wish I knew," Danny said. "But let's give it more time."

They cracked out what little food they had left and ate that, then talked for a short time about how they were going to get from Brazil to Peru. They needed to get to Machu Picchu, if Dr. Hassett's guess about the meaning of the fourth Hydra Journals entry was correct.

Danny had no doubt that the Hydra League also knew that was where they were heading. Danny had no idea what to do about that. Machu Picchu was an ancient city, but the way it sat on top of those mountain ridges, it just wasn't that big a place for five boys to hide from professional killers.

Suddenly, a series of small bangs echoed through the ship, as if someone was firing guns.

Outside the hatch, a few shouts sent them all scrambling back into the dark shadows between the cargo crates.

Then nothing.

Silence. Just the low rumbling of the ships engines and the creaking of the cargo as it shifted slightly in the rolling waves.

No one came through the cargo hatch, no other sounds could be heard.

"I don't like the sound of that," Craig whispered.

Danny didn't either.

"Maybe I should go see what has happened," Bud said.

"No," Danny said. "We wait. The captain will come for us when he can."

"If he can," Craig said.

They all settled in to wait.

Danny sat with his back against a crate at the end of a dark passage. Craig lay stretched out on the deck between two crates to Danny's right, and the twins and Bud were to his left.

Three more hours wore past. Danny was so tired from not sleeping that he kept wanting to close his eyes, but every time he did, he saw hooded men and giant spiders.

Finally, Bud whispered, "We need to know what is happening. It is after five in the evening."

Danny agreed. He pushed himself to his feet, letting his cramped legs stretch out. "I'll go."

All five of them met in the wider area running down the middle between the high-stacked cargo.

"No," Bud said. "I am better at this sort of thing."

"At this point," Craig said, "what difference does it make? They see one of us, they're going to know we're all here. So I say we all go."

Danny glanced at his best friend. "I agree. And we're going to need water and more food soon. There's no way we can last down here the entire trip to South America. We all go."

They turned and headed toward the hatch into the stairway.

It didn't take them long to find out that something was very wrong.

The hatch seemed almost stuck, which got Danny slightly panicked. If they were locked in here, they would die of thirst and hunger long before they reached South America.

He took a deep breath and stepped back.

"Don't tell me we're locked in here?" Craig said, his voice very worried.

"I don't think so," Danny said. "It doesn't feel locked. But there's something on the other side of it. Help me push."

Danny got down low, and then with Craig to his right and Ernie to his left, the three of them pushed on the hatch. It slid open only part way before stopping.

"There's something on the other side," Craig said.

"I can get through that," Bud said, pointing to the slight opening they had managed. "I'll move it."

Bud barely managed to squeeze through, and it took a little more pushing by Danny and Craig on the door to help him get his head through.

Then he vanished.

A moment later, there was a movement on the other side of the door and the hatch swung open.

"Found the problem," Bud said, pointing to the body of a man on the deck as Danny stepped through.

"Is he dead?" Craig asked as he followed Danny.

"Very," Bud said. "Starting to grow cold."

"This can't be good," Craig said.

Danny really hadn't known what he had expected Bud to find, but a body holding the hatch door closed wasn't it. He stared at the man for a moment, trying to understand what he was seeing. If this man had fallen, why hadn't he been discovered before now? Did this have something to do with the bangs and yelling they had heard hours ago?

Then he noticed something.

There was no blood.

And a foam had dried on the dead man's mouth.

"Poisoned," Danny said softly.

39

October 4, 1970
Middle of the South Atlantic

The five of them climbed the stairs out of the cargo hold as silently as they could, finally reaching the lower deck of the ship.

Another man's body lay sprawled in the hallway at the top of the stairs, and again, there was no blood. The guy had just fallen there and died.

"Any idea how many men were on this ship?" Ernie asked, his voice a whisper.

Danny shook his head. "The captain never said."

"More than likely not more than a dozen," Craig whispered. "Counting the captain."

Danny glanced at his best friend with a puzzled look.

Craig shrugged. "I used to think about crewing on one of these cargo ships to get away from home, see the world."

"We need to find the captain," Bud whispered. He pointed up the stairs and Danny nodded.

Bud went first, then Danny followed.

The ship was silent in a way no ship should ever be silent. The engines were still working, the twisting screws sending a vibration through the decks. But nothing else seemed to be making any noise at all.

At the top of the stairs, Bud went right and then into the bridge of the ship.

Danny was right behind him.

The captain and three other men lay dead in the room. They too had clearly been poisoned.

Out the windows, nothing but dark grayish water could be seen in all directions. The sun was low in the sky, coloring a light cloud cover in pinks and reds.

Danny glanced around at the dead men on the bridge, then turned to his friends, who were all staring out over the water as well.

"We need to search the ship and quickly," he said. "Ernie and Ed, take the main deck, search all the rooms, find out what rooms are on that deck as well. Craig and Bud, you take the deck below this one. Make sure you look in every cabin. I'll search this top deck. We meet back here. Be careful."

All of them nodded and headed out.

Danny stared at the sea in front of the ship. From the looks of it, they were all right for the moment. The sea was fairly calm, and the ship seemed to be on some sort of auto-pilot. But they were going to need to find someone alive.

He did a quick search of the top deck and quickly found the communications room. An explosion had torn it completely apart. There was clearly no contacting anyone for help.

The captain's quarters were beyond that, and then a few smaller rooms, including a wine storage area and a small galley stocked with food.

A man in a white chef's uniform was dead on the floor of that room. He clearly had been working on some sort of salad when he died.

Except for a huge map room behind the bridge, that was it for the top deck. Four dead on the bridge, one in the galley.

A few minutes later Bud and Craig appeared.

"Four dead on the second deck," Craig said, his voice soft. He was clearly affected by seeing all this violence.

Danny was as well, but he was trying to not let it get to him. They had to think, and think fast if what he feared was true.

The twins appeared a few minutes later.

"Four dead in the crew's dining room and one in the galley," Ed said.

"So, no one's alive anywhere?" Danny said after telling them what he had found, including how the communications room had been completely destroyed.

"Signs of small explosion on the second deck," Bud said. "And here as well." He pointed to a place under one panel.

Danny looked closely. Clearly, a small explosion had happened there, leaving black stains spraying out over the polished metal.

"Looks like someone must have set off a lot of gas bombs of some sort," Ernie said.

"Unlucky that everyone was inside," Ed said. "If a couple of crew members had been out in the open air, that wouldn't have worked."

"No reason for them to be outside," Craig said, pointing at the deck three stories below the bridge window. "It was a safe bet everyone would be inside and all the killers had to do was make sure the gas was everywhere.

"But why kill this crew?" Bud asked.

Danny looked at his friends, then said, "Hydra League. They must have suspected we were on board somewhere."

"Why not gas the cargo hold as well?" Bud asked.

"No time to set it?" Craig said. "More than likely it was a second search team that was setting the bombs. The captain was with the one that came into the hold."

"So, you're saying they killed this entire ship's crew to kill us?" Ernie asked.

"Considering what they have done so far, it would seem likely," Danny said. "They think they have to stop us somehow."

"Well," Bud said, "whatever the reason this was done, right now we need to get moving and get these bodies outside and toward the stern of the ship."

"Why?" Craig asked.

"I see you've never been around a dead body in the heat," Bud said, staring at Craig.

Craig's face turned white and Danny felt his stomach lurch at just the thought.

Working together, it took them almost an hour to get all the bodies out and onto the stern cargo area. They covered the bodies in a large canvas tarp and tied it down securely.

That was a job that was going to give Danny nightmares for years, if he survived for years.

They gave the crew a moment of silence in respect, then went back up to the bridge.

"Okay, two really important questions," Craig said, staring out over the ocean and the setting sun in front of them. "First, is the food and water poisoned?"

Ernie shook his head. "This was a gas."

"I doubt it would get into anything that was sealed," Ed said.

"Good," Danny said. At least they wouldn't die from starvation.

"Second question, then," Craig said. "We know we're going west, we know we're somewhere in the southern Atlantic. But can anyone drive this thing?"

Silence as they all stared out at the huge ocean as they rode forward through the rolling waves.

"That's what I was afraid of," Craig said.

Danny looked around and then leaned against the map table. "We're on a ghost ship."

40

October 4, 1970
Middle of the South Atlantic

Danny decided after his stomach rumbled loud enough for Craig to comment on it that they all needed to get something to eat and a little rest so that they could think. At the moment they were safe as long as the auto-pilot on the ship stayed on and the Hydra League didn't come back to check on their handiwork.

He mentioned that frightening thought to Bud and they all agreed that they needed to stand watch and stay in the bridge and upper deck for the most part. That way they could see anything approaching.

So Danny sent Bud and Ernie and Ed for food for all of them while he and Craig stayed and stood watch.

The sky had turned from reds and pinks to a dark blue now and the stars had come out.

It was then that Craig said, "We're being followed."

Danny grabbed a pair of binoculars and looked in the direction Craig was pointing. He was right, there was a ship's light there. But it was so far away it was impossible to tell the size of the ship. But it was clearly on the same path they were on.

"Think we could be so lucky and that's another cargo ship?" Craig asked.

Danny shook his head. "Not a chance."

"Think this ship has any weapons on board?" Craig asked.

"Got a feeling we are going to need to find that out right after we eat," Danny said.

"Find out what?" Bud asked as he and Ernie and Ed came back in carrying cans of different food, some plates and silverware, and some jugs of water.

"Weapons?" Craig said. "We are being followed."

"And why does that not surprise me," Bud said.

Danny agreed. Nothing surprised him anymore.

They sat around the big map table eating and talking about options. From what Danny could tell, they had almost none.

Bud came up with the idea of turning off all the ship's lights if they could figure out how to do that.

Danny doubted that would do much good since radar would easily track them.

Craig thought that maybe they could just increase the speed, but none of them were sure that would be a good idea either. Or would serve any real purpose.

So weapons and making the ship their last stand seemed like their only hope. But at least for the moment, the trailing ship didn't seem to be getting any closer. But more than likely by tomorrow morning as the sun gave them light that would change. Danny had no doubt about that.

Absolutely none.

They were on a ghost ship that would soon turn into a battlefield. The five of them would give it a fight, but honestly he didn't give them much hope.

Ed and Ernie took the first watch while Danny, Craig and Bud stretched out in the captain's quarters to sleep for a few hours.

As Danny was falling asleep, all he could think about was his dad. After reading all his notes and such, his dad clearly must have known of the level of pure evil of this Hydra League. Why hadn't he just backed off?

And why were these people so intently set on stopping Danny?

Pieces still didn't make sense and Danny had a hunch they wouldn't until they made it to their next clue.

And more than likely not even then.

41

October 5, 1970
Middle of the South Atlantic

The sun was just starting to show a hint of rising when Craig said, "The ship is getting closer."

It was clear the ship that had been trailing them was small and fast. But that meant it was going to have to get up right against the big cargo ship and the attackers were going to have to climb ropes up the side to get on board.

The five of them had spent hours during the night, after a few hours rest each, either on watch or searching for weapons. They found none. They did find a dozen flare guns in lifeboats and six flares for each gun and some fishing spears of some sort, but that was it. No actual guns at all.

But Danny had no doubt the flare guns could do some real damage, at least at close range. So they each carried one of them. And they stashed the others at specific locations in their defense plan.

They then worked to block or lock all the big metal doors that led up to the top deck. Might as well make it tough for whoever was going to try to kill them to get to them.

Bud had found them an escape route down and out that was mostly a trash chute of some sort, but it would keep them from being trapped up high.

Now all they could do was wait for the other ship to try to board them.

They did have a few lines of attack planned that might slow them down some.

Bud had suggested that they go down on the deck and hide near where someone from the other ship might try to climb up the side and onto the deck. Then when the smaller ship got right below the big ship, the five of them would drop heavy things on the smaller ship.

Danny had liked that idea, even though it got them in the open for gunfire. If they could damage the other boat, it might buy them some time.

Of course, then they would be back to being on a ghost ship. But at the moment that seemed like the best outcome they could hope for.

Craig suggested that once the other smaller boat was close and right against the cargo ship, they could fire some flares into it as well, maybe get lucky and hit something that would catch on fire.

Danny liked that idea as well.

So they had a plan, their fall back final stand in place, their attack set.

Now they just waited as the other ship got closer and closer.

The waiting was pure torture.

They all stayed down and didn't move, expecting the approaching ship to be watching for any signs of life at all.

Within twenty minutes the small craft pulled even with the large cargo ship. Danny and the rest stayed out of sight completely. Anyone near the ship might think they were not on board, so they would have to board to make sure.

The smaller craft fell back and came up the other side, then fell back again and moved in closer to the starboard side.

"Here we go," Danny said to Craig as the ship vanished out of sight down near the waterline of the big cargo ship.

They had figured the boarders would come on board in one of three places with rope ladders affixed to the outside of the tanker and that had been their top pick. So they had stocked everything from heavy footlockers to crates of machine parts and big metal tools that had taken two of them to lift into place.

Bud was the first one to the edge of the ship where the small ship had vanished and peeked over the edge, then quickly scooted back.

"They are tied up against the ship," Bud said. "Right below this point."

He pointed to a spot on the railing.

All of them knew what they had to do.

Danny and Craig grabbed a heavy footlocker and moved it to the edge of the ship and dropped it.

Bud tossed some machine parts over the edge.

The twins picked up a large crate of parts and eased it over the edge.

Bud peeked over and then laughed.

"Direct hits," he said, laughing. "Some big holes in the deck and one guy is down for the count. It's like we kicked a hornet's nest down there."

Danny and Craig quickly eased another footlocker over the edge and gunfire erupted from below, hitting the footlocker just as they released it.

The twins pushed another crate over the edge and Bud cheered.

"Two thugs down."

The gunfire kept coming so they went to just tossing heavy tools over the edge without really exposing themselves.

Then Craig eased up to the edge of the big ship with a flare and fired downward.

"Direct hit," Bud said. "One guy jumped into the water trying to put the flame out."

"How many men are on that thing?" Danny asked, almost afraid to hear the answer.

"Seven more still moving," Bud said.

"Are they going to try to climb up?" Craig asked.

Covering fire opened up from below and Bud ducked back. "I think that is exactly what they are trying right now."

"Craig," Danny said, "move aft and try to get another flare or two into that boat. Ernie, you move toward the stern and do the same."

Both moved quickly, staying low and out of sight of the men below.

"We bomb them with tools," Danny said, grabbing some heavy equipment from some lockers they had found below and sending it over the side.

The three of them kept up a constant rain of heavy metal on the ship and the men trying to climb up.

From both sides both Craig and Ernie fired numbers of flares at the boat and the men.

After the second shot, Danny went ten steps toward the stern and peeked over the edge at the ship going up and down in the rolling waves below.

They had made a mess of the boat, that was for sure.

The small boat was on fire in two places and as he watched, both Ernie and Craig hit it again with more flares. Only two men were left on the small boat still standing, but both were hiding, not even trying to do anything about the fires.

Two men were still on the ropes on the side of the ship, but they seemed to be hanging on for dear life as the rain of metal from above was barely missing them, or clipping them. One looked like he already had a broken shoulder.

Danny took out his flare gun and aimed it at the ropes right above both men.

The flare hit its target and both men went over backwards, one landing in the water and the other hitting the edge of the craft below before bouncing into the water.

The speed of the big cargo ship soon left them behind.

Craig and Ernie again fired into the boat as the two remaining men worked madly to get their boat untied from the larger cargo ship.

Both flares hit targets and both men again ducked for cover.

Two more flares and this time one of the flares hit a gas line and the explosion sent all of them back onto the deck of the cargo ship.

Danny felt like his eyebrows had been singed.

"Wow," Ernie said, shaking his head and trying to clear his ears.

Danny's ears were ringing as well as he scrambled back to the edge to see the small boat below burning.

The small boat was clearly going down.

And fast.

There was no sign of any of the men and most of the boat was on fire.

The five of them watched as after a moment the speed of the cargo ship pushed the nose of the smaller ship under water and then sunk it, ripping it from where it had been tied to the large ship like pulling a loose scab from a wound.

"Holy shit, we did it," Bud shouted.

As Danny stood up, feeling intense relief, a voice behind him laughed and said, "I didn't expect you would need my help."

All five of them spun around, flare guns raised.

The man was smiling, his hands in the air.

It took only a moment for Danny to realize he was staring at his father.

And the next moment he was in his father's arms for the best hug he had ever remembered getting.

And giving.

42

October 5, 1970
Middle of the South Atlantic

The five of them, plus Danny's father, stood around the big map table on the bridge eating and laughing and talking. Bud and the Twins had scrounged up more food and jugs of water and Danny couldn't remember when canned beans and franks had ever tasted so good.

Danny wasn't so sure who was the happiest seeing his father, him or Craig or the twins. Bud seemed to be just taking it all in stride as he always did.

Danny was stunned when he learned that his father had known where they were most of the time, but hadn't been able to get to them ahead of the Hydra men.

And his father was very happy to hear they had copies of his journals and the originals safely hidden back in Cairo.

It seemed that when Danny's father discovered Hydra was coming after him, he vanished, making it seem as if he had been abducted. He had a number of people helping him along the way and when he realized that Hydra was coming after his family and friends as well, he got his wife and brother to safety as soon as his brother got off the plane in Seattle from Cairo.

"We going to be able to see them?" Danny asked.

Danny's father nodded. "As soon as it is safe. They are protected for now."

Danny was very glad to hear that. He hadn't realized how much deep down he had worried about his mother and his uncle until his father said that. He couldn't do anything, so he had just sort of put them out of his mind as much as possible.

"You two just vanished into Cairo," Danny's father said to Danny and Craig. "It was impressive how you did that."

Danny pointed to Bud. "We had expert help."

Bud bowed slightly.

Danny's father went on. "We just couldn't keep up with you five. We were always a half step behind the Hydra men and a full step behind you. Until you ended up here on this ship."

Danny nodded.

He knew that his father had come in on a small craft with a crew of ten and had approached the cargo ship in the shadow, keeping the big ship between him and the Hydra boat. His father and a few others had boarded, fully armed, while Danny and the others fought the Hydra men.

They ate and talked for a few minutes more about the strange fight they had put up and how it had worked even without real weapons.

"The crew of this ship are under tarps on the aft deck," Bud said, reminding them of the deaths of good people who had tried to help them. "Best we could do."

"We'll take care of them before we go," Danny's father said, nodding sadly.

All Danny could do was nod. The captain had given his life and his crew's lives to help them.

"And professor, where exactly are we headed," Ernie asked.

"I would imagine the same place you five were headed," Danny's father said, smiling. "Machu Picchu. And now that we can all work together, I have a hunch we just might be able to solve this puzzle."

"And you want us all along with you?" Bud asked.

"You five solved four pieces of one of the great puzzles of all time," Danny's father said, looking at Danny. "And survived in the process. Of course I want us all working on this together."

Danny looked at his father and he could tell that he wasn't telling the entire truth.

"But you expect the five of us to go one way while you go another," Danny said. "Am I correct?"

"We will need to do that at times," his father said, smiling. "Sometimes teams are better working together, sometimes apart."

"And safer," Bud said, nodding.

Danny didn't like the sound of that at all, not after finally finding his father, but he nodded, then turned to Craig, his best friend. "Do you want to continue on?"

Craig just laughed. "Doing anything else at this point would sound downright boring. I'm in."

Danny smiled and turned to Bud. "There is still treasure out there. You still in?"

"I wouldn't miss this for half the loose change in Cairo," Bud said.

"You two?" Danny asked, turning to the twins.

"We will be honored to be part of this mission and to continue to work with you and the professor," Ernie said for both of them.

Danny turned back to his father, a large smile on his face. "Seems you have more recruits."

"I am honored and thankful," Danny's father said, putting his arm around Danny. "And damn proud of all of you."

Danny just smiled.

"And I want to thank each of you personally for helping Danny look for me," Danny's father said. "It means more than you know."

All of them nodded and Danny felt better and happier than he had felt in memory.

"So now how do we get off this ghost ship?" Bud asked.

Danny glanced at his father, who was smiling, then turned back to Bud. "We don't. At least not yet."

Danny saw his father nodding.

"Did you forget that none of us can run this thing?" Craig asked, sounding shocked.

Danny turned to his father. "I assume you are going to leave a couple men who can operate this cargo ship?"

Again his father nodded. "And fix the radio equipment?"

"Good idea," Bud said.

"They will pose as two crew members who were out in the open when the gas attack hit and on their own got the ship close to port in Brazil. Help will come from the port at that point to finish taking over the ship."

"So why?" Craig asked.

"Because Hydra needs to think we were never on board this ship," Danny said.

Again his father nodded.

"So they will spend their time in South Africa," Ernie said, nodding.

"We can hope," Danny's father said. "But I doubt it will slow them down by too much. But finally they will be behind and that's where we need them."

"Still leaves the question of how we get off?" Bud asked.

"A boat will pick you up in the middle of the night one day off the coast of Brazil," Danny's father said. "That will get you to shore and from there you need to make your way to Machu Picchu. Money and equipment and supplies will be waiting for you as well as transportation around the tip and up the South American coastline."

"So when will we see you again?" Danny asked.

"I have to get more help for this cause," Danny's father said. "This will be a very long fight ahead of us and we have to be ready to win this before any of us can truly be safe."

Danny just nodded. He felt ready now for anything that might come their way. And knowing his father was out there working toward the same end calmed him more than he wanted to admit.

So two hours later, Danny stood with his best friends on the deck of the cargo ship in the wind and the setting daylight and watched the small ship carrying his father vanish off ahead of them.

The two men from his father's team were already working on the radio and correcting the ship's course to get it back solidly in the shipping lanes.

When the small boat could no longer be seen, Danny turned to his four friends. "Thank you. We set out to find my father and we did. And I can't thank you enough."

"Technically he found us," Bud said and Craig punched him lightly.

They all laughed and to Danny that laugh felt wonderful.

"So what are we supposed to do for the next ten days until we get off this monster?" Bud asked.

"I think we might want to study the journals more," Danny said.

Craig and the twins nodded.

"We might as well be as ready as we can be for what's coming," Craig said.

"Exactly," Danny said. "And whatever it is, I have a hunch it will be exciting."

"And that might be the greatest understatement of the century," Bud said.

Danny had no doubt that was the truth.

And he found that exciting.

As long as he now knew his father was alive and working with them. That really was all that mattered.

If you enjoyed Danny Hawk and *The Adventures of Hawk*, you might also like Buffalo Jimmy. What follows is a sample chapter from *Headed West: The Life and Times of Buffalo Jimmy*.

The first shot ripped into nineteen-year-old Jimmy Gray's saddle with a sickening thud, barely missing his right leg.

The sound of the shot echoed over the rolling Missouri hills and died into the clear, sunny afternoon air. His horse reared and threatened to bolt even though the shot had not gone through the thick leather, but Jimmy fought it back into control, spinning around completely on the ridgeline covered by prairie grass.

A second shot knocked Jimmy's brother, Luke, off his horse.

Jimmy dove for the ground and cover as a third shot narrowly missed him, the sound of the bullet whistling past his ear.

He lay on the ground, face pressed into the soft dirt and grass, trying to breathe. His heart was racing. He had never been so scared in all his life.

He had never been shot at before. He read about such things in dime novels and in the newspapers, but reading about it and having it happen to you were two very different things.

Jimmy and his family were two days ride from Independence, Missouri. He and his brother had just come over the ridge two hundred paces above their family's wagon. Five men had been down there near the back of the wagon, off their horses, from what Jimmy could tell in the quick glimpse before the shooting had started

He hadn't seen his parents.

That scared him even more than being shot at. He just hoped they weren't hurt.

And was Luke hurt? He had to find out.

He had to move.

Jimmy couldn't believe this was even happening. All Jimmy had wanted to see was buffalo. Since his teacher a year ago back in Boston, in his last year of high school, had told him stories of the great buffalo hunts, Jimmy had been focused on little else. The big beasts had become an obsession, his mother had said. His father had only laughed and promised that Jimmy would see his share of buffalo by the time they reached the Wyoming Territory.

His older brother, Luke, had told him as they rode out of camp that the buffalo were no longer in Missouri in 1866, at least not this part of it. They had all been killed or driven hundreds of miles away from the wagon trail, but Jimmy didn't care. He still had his mind set on seeing a buffalo and proving Luke wrong. For all he knew, there could be an entire herd just over the next ridge.

After riding fast away from the well-worn wagon road for a half-mile or so, they had scared up rabbits. Luke, who was twenty, had the family rifle. He had become a great shot and had managed to get three rabbits with only five shots. Jimmy was an expert shot as well. Once

Luke even had admitted he was better than Luke, a real natural with a gun.

Jimmy had helped Luke skin the rabbits and then they had headed back. Luke had been sick since leaving St. Louis and was riding slowly. Jimmy could tell that both of his parents were worried about Luke making the long trip across the country, but Jimmy' father had a job offer at a bank in San Francisco, and had bought a gold mining claim in the mountains near Sacramento, so the family was set on making the trip and starting a new life in the west.

It had been such a perfect, spring day.

Until the shots.

What had happened?

Jimmy scrambled on all fours through the grass, his head low, until he finally managed to reach his brother.

Luke was pushing himself up slightly on his elbows and blood was streaming from his leg. "Get the rifle off my saddle," he said through gritted teeth. "Quick!"

Jimmy glanced around.

Luke's horse had only gone about twenty paces back from the top of the ridge and then stopped. Keeping his head down, Jimmy ran for the horse, grabbed the rifle from the saddle and brought it back.

There were no more shots at him coming from their wagon, but off his horse, Jimmy couldn't see the trail over the edge of the rise, which meant the men doing the shooting couldn't see him.

Luke had torn off the bottom of his shirt and wrapped it around his leg, but it didn't look to Jimmy as if the bleeding had slowed much.

Luke grabbed the rifle from Jimmy, cocked it to make sure it was loaded, then staying low, hopped the few steps to the top of the ridge, dragging his bad leg behind him.

Jimmy stayed beside him, and at the top of the ridge they both lay down in the grass and crawled the last few feet so they could see the trail below.

Jimmy was shocked at what faced them. He wanted to jump and run, but somehow stayed beside Luke.

Two men on horseback were riding up the hill toward them, guns drawn. Three other men were pulling things from the wagon and scattering them on the ground. Jimmy had no idea where his parents were.

He and Luke were going to die, Jimmy was sure of that.

This was just like all the bad stories he had heard about the western frontier coming true right now.

His stomach was so twisted up, he could hardly breathe.

"Keep your head down," Luke whispered.

Then, taking a deep breath, Luke pulled down on the men like he was shooting rabbits. The shot exploded in Jimmy's ear, since he was so close to Luke.

The lead man went over backwards off his horse like a trick rider Jimmy had seen at the Circus last year in Boston.

The other man's horse reared up, and by the time he could get turned around, Luke fired again.

He must have missed. The second man took off back down the hill toward the wagon. The man that Luke had shot pushed himself to his feet, holding his stomach, and then half-ran, half-staggered back down the hill.

The three men below had their guns out and were firing up at Luke and Jimmy.

"Keep your head down," Luke ordered again. Then he fired back at the men around the wagon. Jimmy watched one of Luke's shots splinter wood off the wagon bed right beside one man.

Luke shot again and another of the men danced as the bullet kicked up dirt and mud right at his feet.

Luke didn't hit any of the men, but his next shot, and the one after, sent them scrambling for their horses.

Jimmy recognized one of the men.

Jake Benson, the man his father had hired to guide them from St. Louis to Independence.

The three men quickly mounted up and joined the fourth. He had picked up the wounded man and was riding at full speed down the trail toward Independence. The horse of the man Luke had shot grazed on the side of the hill. Clearly, they didn't have the stomach for a fight in the open for a horse with Luke having the rifle and the upper ground and all they had were pistols.

Jimmy watched them go, their dust kicking up small clouds behind them.

It seemed to take an eternity for them to vanish over the distant rise.

When would they be back? The question made Jimmy shudder.

The wagon still sat where Jimmy and Luke had left it when they had left to go hunting. It was sitting just off to one side of the muddy tracks of the wagon road, with their two secondary horses grazing while still in harness. But the lunch fire was smoldering instead of burning, and a lot of their personal things had been tossed out into the dirt and dried mud.

After all the shooting, the silence of the wide-open prairie was broken only by the light breeze through the grass.

Tomb-like silent.

Luke sat up, checked his wound, then pushed himself to his feet.

"Get our horses," he said to Jimmy.

Jimmy turned and ran for their two horses, the fear of what might have happened to his parents twisting at his stomach like a bad belly-ache. He grabbed Luke's horse, then mounted up on his own, the hole where the bullet had embedded in the leather of his saddle a clear reminder of just how close he had come to getting shot.

By the time he got back to his brother, Luke's face looked white, and it was clear that he was in a lot of pain.

"Let's find Mother and Father," Luke said, reaching for his horse's reins.

Jimmy made sure Luke could get back on his horse, then started down the hill ahead of his older brother, working to keep his hands from shaking and his stomach under control while trying to look in a thousand directions at the same time for Benson and his men. They would be back. He had no doubt.

The wind whistled lightly in his ears under his hat, the warm afternoon sun glared in his eyes. He forced himself to take shallow breaths as the ride seemed to stretch into an eternity.

It wasn't until he had moved almost halfway down the hill that he saw what he had feared the most. His mother and father were lying in the mud near the rear wheels of the wagon. Neither seemed to be moving.

Jimmy dismounted ten running steps from the wagon before the horse had even stopped.

An instant later he was on his knees beside his father.

He was dead.

His blood had made a muddy pool, his eyes were staring up, unseeing at the blue sky and light white clouds. He had been shot at least twice.

Jimmy stared at the man who had always been there for him. His father couldn't be dead. He was too strong, too powerful a man to die.

An instant later, Luke was on the ground beside their mother.

Jimmy watched as Luke rolled her over. The front of her pretty blue dress was coated in mud and her own blood.

She had been shot in the back.

As Luke rolled her over, she blinked, then opened her eyes.

She was alive!

For a moment, it was clear she wasn't aware of where she was, but as Jimmy moved closer, she looked up at Luke.

"Mother?" Luke said, his voice shaking.

Jimmy touched her arm, trying to give her some comfort as well. He had no idea what they could do.

"Benson," she whispered. "Hide from him."

"He's not here," Luke said. "We chased him and his men off."

She nodded, seemingly satisfied with that. She coughed, blood coming out of the corner of her mouth. She looked up at Jimmy and smiled, then back at Luke. "Take care of each other."

Jimmy watched as she closed her eyes and her body relaxed.

All the life seemed to leave her.

"Mother!" Luke shouted, his voice swallowed by the vast wilderness around them.

Their mother was dead.

They were alone.

Newsletter sign-up

Be the first to know!

Just sign up for the Dean Wesley Smith newsletter, and keep up with the latest news, releases and so much more—even the occasional giveaway.

So, what are you waiting for? To sign up go to deanwesleysmith.com.

But wait! There's more. Sign up for the WMG Publishing newsletter, too, and get the latest news and releases from all of the WMG authors and lines, including Kristine Kathryn Rusch, Kristine Grayson, Kris Nelscott, *Fiction River: An Original Anthology Magazine, Smith's Monthly,* and so much more.

To sign up go to wmgpublishing.com.

ABOUT THE AUTHOR

Considered one of the most prolific writers working in modern fiction, *USA Today* bestselling writer Dean Wesley Smith published far more than a hundred novels in forty years, and hundreds of short stories across many genres.

At the moment he produces novels in several major series, including the time travel Thunder Mountain novels set in the Old West, the galaxy-spanning Seeders Universe series, the urban fantasy Ghost of a Chance series, a superhero series starring Poker Boy, and a mystery series featuring the retired detectives of the Cold Poker Gang.

His monthly magazine, *Smith's Monthly*, which consists of only his own fiction, premiered in October 2013 and offers readers more than 70,000 words per issue, including a new and original novel every month.

During his career, Dean also wrote a couple dozen *Star Trek* novels, the only two original *Men in Black* novels, Spider-Man and X-Men novels, plus novels set in gaming and television worlds. Writing with his wife Kristine Kathryn Rusch under the name Kathryn Wesley, he wrote the novel for the NBC miniseries The Tenth Kingdom and other books for *Hallmark Hall of Fame* movies.

He wrote novels under dozens of pen names in the worlds of comic books and movies, including novelizations of almost a dozen films, from *The Final Fantasy* to *Steel* to *Rundown*.

Dean also worked as a fiction editor off and on, starting at Pulphouse Publishing, then at *VB Tech Journal*, then Pocket Books, and now at WMG Publishing, where he and Kristine Kathryn Rusch serve as series editors for the acclaimed *Fiction River* anthology series.

For more information about Dean's books and ongoing projects, please visit his website at www.deanwesleysmith.com and sign up for his newsletter.

For more information:
www.deanwesleysmith.com